SEARCHING *FOR* Sula

by Tracey L. DeBrew

herwritehand publishing, Inc
Washington, DC

Paperback First Edition 2012

Library of Congress Cataloging Number
available upon request

ISBN-13: (Pbk)
978-0-9832492-1-4

to Mom & Dad -
thanks for supporting my (writing) habit

Chapter One - My Journey

I try my best not to follow everyone's rules, especially my own. Rules are for people who are disciplined and like decency and order. I tried that. I constantly draw up guidelines for myself, which I seldom stick to. When I was much younger I was a rebel. If someone said go right, I would purposely go left – just to see if I was missing anything. Now that I'm quickly approaching thirty, I'm realizing that order keeps me sane. I made a list of things that I wanted to do before 30. Oh well, the list needs to be revisited because my broke behind didn't have the money to do most of the stuff on that list. What was I thinking? Speaking of approaching 30, I've noticed that my body is also changing and not for the better.

I've gotten a little more exhausted when crossing the street, a little more winded when walking up only a single flight of stairs, and I'm more likely to bed down by

9 p.m., rather than 4 a.m. like I did when I was in college. As I approach my third decade on earth, the bitter truth is it's time to grow up, give back to society in some charitable way, and by God, find a faithful husband and settle down.

Yes sports fans, this is what it's boiled down to. The missing piece of the puzzle to complete the package called Sula Tyler. My mother named me after the lead character in Toni Morrison's book "Sula". She said it was quite befitting for me once I hit my teens. As I said, I grew up reserved then I became wild in my teens, which made me a mysterious young lady to her. Most of this resonated in my art.

I'm a non-starving artist who perfected my craft at Texas A&M where I majored in Art History. Well, not quite "perfected", I'm talented...I guess. Honestly, I suck. I have created several pieces that remain in storage because I'm too afraid to display anything, let alone ask people to buy it. I'm sure I will someday. I just need some new inspiration. After a few months of floundering after graduating from Texas, I went back to get my Master's in Arts & Sciences. After school, I had the pleasure of working for a fine art gallery in New Orleans.

Being surrounded with so many paintings from a wide array of artists like Charles Bibbs, Salvador Dali, and Monet was equivalent to Christmas in July. Art allowed me to runaway and it took me to the tiny piece of the artist's world that they so generously recreated on canvas. It was my dream job until I moved to Portland, Oregon.

I worked hard for a magazine publisher as an assistant editor, and was promoted to senior editor just after six months of being hired by the company. After two and a half years of loyal service, they laid my ass off. There was no inclination of a merger, and no clue that I wasn't needed anymore. The joys of capitalism.

After feeling like I had been used by corporate America, I up and headed for D.C. I thought it would be a great place to settle in for business purposes. The clientele could range from a college student to a Senator. By the time I moved across country to D.C., I had no idea that the area was also overflowing with successful men. Too bad, because I moved to D.C. to be closer to my boo. It was love at its finest. After only a few years in D.C., I've permanently given up trying to figure out the male species.

Take Lawrence. He's a cool guy with equal attributes, but he cringes at the mere thought of commitment. He's sweet, but simple-minded at times. I often take second when it comes to a boxing match starring fighters I've never heard of before, college games and any other sporting event from football to cribbage. Cribbage? Really? Don't get me wrong, I love to watch a good game of football and basketball occasionally, but enough becomes enough after a while.

Not Lawrence.

If he could, he'd have a remote that was programmed to ESPN, CSN, and HTS glued to his right hand and his left hand would be shoved down the front of his pants. I wasn't really sure why I put up with it and suppose that's why we became an off again more than an on again kind of couple. His actions often made me evaluate what our love affair was, or even if it *was* love.

Today was Thursday and after his ritual night of hanging with the fellas, he often stopped by for a night cap. When Lawrence walked in my apartment, he was looking and smelling as good as usual. He was about three inches taller than me at six feet, had a fantastic toasted brown complexion, with boyish eyes that danced, and the warmest smile. He had a basketball player's physique and was well put together "down there." He gave me a kiss and came on inside.

"Hey sweetie," he said and took a seat on the couch. He held his hand up to beckon me over and smiled. Just like a lovesick woman, I trotted right on over and took my rightful place on his lap. He massaged my shoulder with one hand and got right to the point.

"How long we been together now?" he asked.

"Almost two years. You know that. It was your suggestion that I move here to be closer to you."

"Oh yeah, it was," he said looking around at my artwork. "That meant a lot to me that you would do that, baby. Move from Portand to be with little ol' me. I knew you truly loved me."

"Yes, I'm glad we kept in contact when you left Portland. I hated to see you go. And it was right when our relationship was getting good," I admitted.

"But you came shortly after and kept it alive!"

This was sounding like a lead in to an extremely important conversation - the type of conversation that could change our lives forever. I wanted to take in every aspect of this moment. What he wore, how he looked, and his scent. After all, I would be telling this story to our grandchildren and did not want to miss any of the small details. As I sat comfortably on his lap, my eyes darted anxiously around the room. I expected a brass band to come barging into my house along with some tuxedoed man carrying flowers and champagne. I wanted to yell out, *"Yes! Yes! I'll marry you!"* Instead, I put on my prettiest face and listened intently.

"Sula, I want to ask you something," he started.

"Yes, baby?" *Here it goes*, I thought. I stroked the back of his neck gently with the tips of my fingers and waited to hear what he was about to ask. I took a deep breath to regulate my fluttering heart and then smiled.

"How would you like it if we dated other people?"

"Oh you've made me so happy!" I blurted without hearing his question fully.

Lawrence smirked and jerked his head slightly back as he brandished a confused expression.

"What?" he asked.

"Wait," I said as my smile dissipated, "um, you didn't ask me to marry you."

He snickered before he said, "Uhhh, no. I didn't."

"Hold up. What did you ask me?"

"Sula, I asked you if we could see other people," he said as he patted my back.

"Get the hell off!" I said as I jumped up from his lap.

"Sula?"

"How would I like it?" I asked, "I wouldn't! When did you decide you wanted to see other people?"

"Well, I just thought that maybe I was smothering you and you may have wanted to see other guys. I don't want to tie you down, you know?"

"Did I ever tell you I wanted to see other guys?"

"No, but..."

"So what are you talking about?" I flopped down on the couch and shook my head in disbelief. It felt as though the walls were closing in on me as his words pecked at my mind like a nagging headache. Instead of answering my question, he stood in front of me anticipating some type of reaction. So I gave his ass one.

I ran into the bedroom and pulled out a huge suitcase. I began grabbing clothes from the dresser drawers and slammed them inside their new Samsonite home.

"What are you doing?" he asked as he watched my frantic packing.

"What does it look like, fool? I'm packing."

"I see that, but baby where are you going?"

"*Back* to Texas! Why do you care?"

"Sula, I *do* care about you, but right now I'm just not sure about the two of us."

"You were sure about us last night when I was riding you and you were yelling my damn name!"

Lawrence threw his head back at the comment and sighed. I ripped open my closet door and began yanking clothes off of the hangers. I almost mowed him over in my anger because he was directly in my path; just standing there watching as if I were starring in a Broadway stage play. This mofo was cutting me off after I had spent nearly two years of *my* precious time? *This* is the pay-off? Give me a break.

"You wanna break up. Why? Why now?" I demanded to know.

He chuckled lightly. Afterward his devilish smirk remained. "It's not like this was planned or timed." He grabbed my hand, but I yanked it away. Then I wondered what he thought was so damn funny.

"You think this is some game, Lawrence? You're playing with people's emotions now?"

"Of course not, baby."

"Don't call me, baby! I can't believe that after all this time you want to break up?"

"Not break up, just have a little space. You know, take a little break," he rubbed his palms together nervously.

"What the hell does take a little break and have a little space mean? Oh no! I can't believe I trusted you, Lawrence. Oh!" I rubbed my forehead to calm my nerves. I could feel the lump forming in my throat and the urge to shed several tears. I swallowed that slab of rejection and refused to give him the satisfaction. Then I begin to feel like a fool for moving to D.C. "Oh God, how am I gonna trust you again? Well no, not you. *Anyone* again?"

"Sula . . ." he started.

"So, who is she?" I had stopped packing just long enough to hear his response.

"What?" his voice changed as if the notion of him being with someone else was preposterous.

"Never mind. I don't care! I'm outta here. And you? You get out!"

I closed the suitcase, clothes spilling out from its sides, and hauled it out of the bedroom with Lawrence bearing down on my heels. He stood in front of me to stop my tirade.

"It's not you, Sula, you're great. It's me. I want to be everything I can be for you. And I don't feel like I am right now."

"You're right, you're not. Goodbye, Lawrence," I put on my coat and held the door open for him and myself.

Lawrence was supposed to be my soul mate and somewhere in our relationship, I had become content. I noticed no differences. Everything appeared fine. It was as if I was reliving being laid off from the magazine all over again. The element of surprise always yields confusion and feelings of inadequacy. I sincerely hoped he wasn't throwing away all of the good times we shared just to have a roll in the sack with some woman.

"You're not going to Texas. Where are you going? Will you tell me that?"

"I need to find myself, Lawrence. I got so wrapped up into you that I got lost. Goodbye."

Lawrence shuffled slowly toward the door and waited for a few seconds. He appeared to be in deep thought as the tension hung heavily in the air. After several seconds, he doubled back and tried to give me a kiss on the cheek. I looked away instead. I just could not look into his eyes anymore, because there housed his lies and deceit. He wanted some response to his affection, but there was none to be offered. Once he realized that, he left. The sound of the door closing behind him sounded like the lid of a coffin and my heart was trapped inside. In one movement, I collapsed to the floor and wept.

After my meltdown and poor attempt to put the pieces of my heart back together, I hopped in my car and sped to the airport. I safely eluded police after running several red lights and driving 80 miles per hour. As the tears streamed down my cheeks, I refused to be the poor little desperate rejected girl who couldn't keep a man. I looked good and considered myself to be a good catch for any decent self-respecting male. The truth was, it *wasn't* me, it was him, just like he suggested. On my journey to wherever, I would have another good cry, a session of reflection, then pick myself up, dust myself off and move what they call, the hell on.

When I arrived at National Airport, I looked at all of the ticketing agents and the airlines they were representing. Jamaica? No, my name wasn't Stella. Bahamas? Not far enough. Vegas? I needed to get *out* of the country. Aruba? Hell no, too many people go there and never make it back.

Then I spotted this adorable little girl who looked to be about five years old. She had the fattest cheeks I'd seen on a child and thinly twisted locks that covered her back. Her mother wore a dark brick red oversized shawl that draped her head and body. As she turned to call her child, the scarf fell from her head to reveal her thin locks pulled neatly into a bun. The youngster looked in my direction, waved and ran over to her mother. Before they boarded their flight, the youngster turned again and stared in my direction, and then disappeared around the corner.

I strolled up to the counter and stood boldly in front of the ticket agent.

"Yes, I'd like to go to Africa," I demanded of the agent.

"Do you have a flight number or an e-ticket?" she asked.

"No, sorry."

"You *do* realize the cost for a flight to Africa without prior booking, correct?"

I glared at her and ignored her question. She clicked the keys on her monitor for a moment and then clicked some more. I wiped away more tears as I waited for the price my account would be liable for. She handed me a tissue from behind her station and gave an empathetic smile.

"Well, you're in luck. There has been a cancellation. They relinquished the round trip flight, safari tour package, meals and hotel stay. It's for two weeks, but the flight is Thursday of next week. Is that fine?"

I nodded and sniffed.

"Okay," she typed some more. "That will be $4,843." She looked up at me with a fearful expression. I guess she supposed I would bawl louder once I heard the price and retreat with my head hanging low. Instead, I slammed my platinum card down on the counter.

"Charge it."

*   *   *   *

While I was in the doctor's office getting all of the necessary vaccinations for my departure, I considered the many rules of the dating game. Although Lawrence didn't admit he had cheated, what else could it have been? We never argued, we spent time apart and plenty of time together, the sex was great…what could it have been? Now all of a sudden he needs space? To me, space translated into break up. It had to be another woman.

After being dumped by Lawrence, I felt like I was back at square one and upset with myself. The time I wasted with Lawrence could've been given to someone who was serious about having a future with me. I needed some time to reflect and I suppose I needed to draft some new guidelines. Assuredly, these guidelines would yet again not be followed by me. Why do I constantly do that? That will be one of the questions I will have to ask myself when I'm on vacation in about a week.

Anyway, I am on my way to East Africa.

Chapter Two - Africa

I stopped by the bookstore and found several books on East Africa. I did a final check to make sure I had packed everything I would need for the next two weeks. There would be a lot of clothing reruns because I wanted to pack light. I curled up with one of the books I had purchased, but I didn't read it. Instead my eyes just passed over the words. I thought about how things were before I left Texas – when I knew the difference between true love and simple infatuation. Even though I was young, I was in love back then. Those days, joyous and painful, I kept buried in my distant memory – in a place deep within my heart, never to be seen again.

I arrived at the airport that Thursday. Exactly one week after Lawrence tossed me aside like a used Kleenex. I wasn't looking forward to traveling for the next 2 days, but I was definitely glad that I would be spending that time away from the U.S. My arms and tush were just healing from all of the shots administered by the doctor before I could leave the country. I packed enough junk food for an entire village, along with puzzle books, word games, novels, and magazines to help pass the time. I'd even stashed away some Dramamine – extra drowsy – in my purse.

When I boarded the connector flight in Doha, Qatar for the last leg of the trip, I popped another Dramamine and was off to sleep in an hour. Before I knew it, we were about to begin our descent into Kenya. After I awoke and shook off the effects of the drugs, I peered out of the window and noticed a huge mountain which had to be Mt. Kilimanjaro. I couldn't believe that in a matter of minutes, I would actually be in Africa! I would taste their food, experience their culture, visit their popular spots, trade stories with the locals and have plenty of stories to share once I got home. A warm joyous tear streaked down my cheek. I couldn't take my eyes off of the scenery below.

I gathered my bags quickly in a rush to leave the airport and touch the soil of Africa with my own two feet. When I made it outside, I dropped my bags, knelt down, and kissed the hot asphalt with my lips. I felt like I had returned home.

The natives were some of the friendliest people I'd ever met. I sat toward the front of the bus to get a better view of where we were going. The bus driver suggested that after I drop my bags off at the hotel to go on a safari.

He asked the often repeated question, "Where are you from?"

"D.C." I answered automatically not thinking of where I was born, but where I currently resided.

"Washington?" he asked.

"Yes, have you been there?"

"No. I will go. Well, maybe New York first."

"Of course," I replied flatly. "Can you tell me about Narok?"

"Oh yes, it is near the Maasai Village. There is an entrance fee of four American dollars to take pictures in the village. You can buy lots of carvings, but if you want beadwork, Tanzania is best. Are you traveling by yourself?"

I stared out of the window at the plains and elaborate view of the mountains. Once I left the states, I hadn't given Lawrence a thought until he asked me about traveling alone.

"Yes, I am," I said with a lighthearted sigh.

*   *   *   *

My cottage was one of several perched on a hillside that over looked the valley. I stared out as I caught a glimpse of the sun beginning to set. I decided to call one of my friends to tell them that I had made it safely.

"Kaye, it's Sula," I began. She screamed in my ear when she heard my voice.

"Suuuulllaaa! You made it okay? How is it? I wish I was there with you, but I couldn't take off to Africa at a moment's notice like *some* people."

"Don't even try it. I'm safe, call Vanessa for me."

"No problem. You know I'm expecting some serious souvenirs from your little road trip to the Motherland."

"Yeah, yeah, I'll call you again soon."

The cool wind caressed the white sheer curtains as I lay on the bed, listening to the different sounds of the night that I wasn't accustomed to from living in the city. I drifted off to sleep.

I woke up a little after four in the morning; my body had not yet adjusted to the time change. I prepared for the day and my trip to the Maasai Village according to the itinerary. I packed my camera bag and stuffed four SD cards and 12 AA batteries inside. I secured my hiking boots and pulled my ponytail through the back of my cap.

I was crunching on some Cheez-Its that were left over from my munchies survival pack and watching the local news when there was a knock on my door around seven. I went to the door to see who it could be. It was a short portly man dressed in all white.

"Yes?"

"We'll be leaving in thirty minutes. Do you have your tools for tomorrow?"

"My tools?" I looked at portly rather strangely.

"Yes, we are doing carpentry work for the dorm rooms at the new college starting tomorrow."

"No one told me about bringing tools. What exactly are we building?" I tried to plaster a smile on my face. I was by no means a handyman.

"Drawers, desks and bookshelves. Not to worry, there will be extra tools there."

I nodded as his perfectly accented diction hovered in the humid air. I thought about what this possibly meant to this country. It could be the first college in the area, or an expansion to a neighboring school. It would be an honor. I smiled and patted his shoulder.

"Okay, I'll be ready tomorrow."

*   *   *   *

The Maasai were herd's people who lived in a village that consisted of about 20 huts enclosed by what I later found out to be Acacia bushes, which had long thorns in them. They were used to ward off animals and outsiders.

An English speaking young Maasai warrior named Aderele, showed my group around the village. His skin was so smooth, clear and richly dark. Not to mention he was so tall and lean, that I considered altering my diet once I got back into the states.

The tourist had gathered around Aderele while he spoke. Observing my surroundings, I turned my attention to one of the huts directly behind us. There was a partially opened cloth covering the entrance. Instinctively, I turned completely around to face the hut and before I knew it, I was walking toward it. It seemed as though something stronger than just curiosity was guiding me to go over. I peeked inside and there was an old blind woman, sitting on a tree stump covered by animal hides. A young girl of about twelve years old was standing next to her. The old woman said something to me in their native dialect, Maa, but of course I didn't understand her. The young girl told me to sit down on the ground. A tinge of fear now over powered the curiosity I experienced. I did not feel as though I would be scolded for intruding, but felt welcomed.

"This is my great great grandmother," the girl told me. "She is very old, but wise. She cannot see, but says that you have traveled a great distance in search of something."

"Yes," I responded.

The old woman spoke again this time in a short clipped tone. Her hair was full and white, just like her blinded eyes.

"She says you are making a mistake," the young girl translated.

"Excuse me?"

The woman spoke again this time only longer. I listened to her dialect as if I understood every word. When she was done, I looked to her granddaughter for the translation.

"She says you choose not to be in love again because of your last love. Denying love will cause you much pain and sorrow. But if you choose to explore love again, there will be three suitors. You do not choose your mates wisely but she will help you."

"I don't understand. How could she . . .?"

The old woman handed me a bracelet woven from smoothed antelope hide, from what the granddaughter told me. I was instructed to wear the bracelet the entire time I was in Africa. When I got back to the states, she told me to put on the bracelet after I met a new man who expressed interest in me, but whom I was also attracted to. I was to keep it on all night while I slept and remove it right after I awoke. That was a lot of instructions! The hide, which was soaked in a bowl of divine water, would help me see the men clearly for who they were. I wasn't quite sure what any of it meant, but for her to be so old and to tell me right off the bat that I was making a mistake resonated with me. I was prepared to do whatever she said at that point. I hugged them, told them both goodbye and met back up with my tour group.

My timing was perfect because, a wedding celebration was about to start. Food was being prepared away from the village, which Aderele told me we would be able to taste. I nervously rubbed the bracelet on my wrist as I watched the Maasai men and women gather for the wedding ceremony. They wore red cloth and lots of beads around their necks and feet. By the time the ceremony was underway, I had already filled an SD card on my camera. The couple to be wed couldn't have been anymore than fourteen or fifteen. I was experiencing a part of my ancestry from hundreds of years ago, but in many ways I felt so far separated from them.

After our visit there, we went on the safari tour in Mara. When our truck parked, I pulled out my camera and knew I'd be taking about another hundred to two hundred photos. There were plenty of zebras, wildebeests, and gazelles waiting for me to capture them in their habitat. We drove up further to the watering hole and saw several impala, giraffe, exotic birds and of course, elephants.

The tour guide pointed out a cheetah perched in the high grass looking out over the animals. Where there's a cheetah, there were bound to be lions nearby. The experience was indescribable and I know my photos did not do it much justice.

The next day, we made a lot of furniture for the college. I wasn't expecting to do any manual labor on this trip, but after all, it was a cancellation. I felt overly proud after I made my first desk. I stood back and admired my handy work as I guzzled a cold bottle of water. Afterward, we went to Nairobi and ate at some restaurant called Carnivore. It was like a Brazilian steakhouse, but with more exotic meat choices. The way it worked was the waiters come around with different kinds of meat on a skewer. If you're interested, they hack a piece off and dump it onto your plate. This will continue all night if the food indicator light is green. Once it is switched to red, the meat ceases and the consumer gets a chance to loosen their belt and/or undo some buttons. I had zebra, ostrich, giraffe, crocodile and hartebeest. I felt a little uneasy that I was chowing down on some of the very species that I had taken photos of earlier that day. They were tasty though! I felt at home in Kenya, although this wasn't where I grew up. Complete would be the word I would use to describe the feeling I had at the end of these two weeks. I also had a renewed sense of direction toward my life. This trip forced me to make several adjustments when I returned to the States, which I was ready to apply and share with my girls back home.

Chapter Three - My Homies

My girl Kaye is my confidante. She has an answer for everything – sometimes good, sometimes bad. She can make me laugh until I cry or make me laugh when I'm crying. Kaye is the type of person that has fun no matter where she is. Persuasive as hell, Kaye can charm a person into buying their dirty underwear if given the chance. Kaye was that girl we all knew in high school – the witty, charming, intelligent, and oh so sweet captain of the cheerleading squad. Kaye is what I call statuesque; she has the body women pay thousands in plastic surgery bills to mimic. There is a lot to be said for good genes. She has a beautiful face, and always smiles to show off her dimples. Everywhere we go men and women stare at her, some to admire her beauty and others to figure out her beauty secrets.

Kaye always spoke her mind and said what she wanted, when she wanted. Sometimes it would be tactful and sometimes it wouldn't. It all depended on the mood she was in.

Despite her outlandish behavior, Kaye spends much of her spare time volunteering at a homeless shelter and tutors adults in reading and math who are trying to get their GED.

Now my other friend, Vanessa, is the exact opposite of Kaye. She's the baby sister I never had, even though she's older than me. Vanessa acts like the quiet withdrawn type - only after a rejection or heartbreak. We aren't best friends, but if she needed help, I'd be there. I think she would do the same for me, at least I hope she would. Sometimes I wouldn't see Vanessa for weeks and weeks at a time. I may talk to her once a week if she isn't cocooning. Even though she sometimes acts withdrawn, that doesn't fool me. I've seen her in action and she absolutely loves the attention of men. The ironic part is that Vanessa will do anything to get their attention, but it's never the right attention. She will catch on one of these days.

Vanessa has a full voluptuous shape and is probably a size 16. Vanessa's biggest problem is she thinks all men like women who wear a size six or below. *Whatever!*

Vanessa would be surprised at how many fellas would be lined up to take her out if she would just spruce up her wardrobe and not be so clingy. Vanessa was a homebody by choice and the club scene wasn't her thing.

She would often pass on a lot of our girl's night out invitations; however, she never declined going out with us to eat or grab a drink.

Wondering about me? I've been told that I resemble a darker version of Nicole Ari Parker, the actress that played 'Teri' on the drama *Soul Food*. And the number one question I'm asked is, "are those your real eyes?" If I had a dollar every time someone asked me that, I'd already have a piece of beachfront property in Cancun, using the left over money to sip on some wine coolers. That is one of the rudest questions anyone could ask, just short of "Is that your real hair?" I guess sisters can't be born with hazel eyes and a full head of hair anymore.

My body has a decent shape, but I could stand to lose a few more pounds. In college I gained the freshman 15 and then some. The pounds stayed with me longer than the average boyfriend. Since then, I've lost 20 pounds and worked hard to keep the weight off. My reward was a fierce new wardrobe.

Friday night will actually be the first time Kaye, Vanessa and I will all be hanging out at a club. For me and Kaye, clubbing was nothing new. As a matter of fact, she and I went out the week before I got dumped by Lawrence. I'm just wondering what Vanessa will wear, because I have never seen her in anything other than business clothes, tee shirts and sweats.

*   *   *   *

We decided to meet at my house to have a drink before heading out to the club. Kaye paced the length of my living room as she clutched her glass of chardonnay.

The clink from her ring on the side of the crystal stemware imitated her eagerness to get to the club.

"What's taking homegirl so long?" Kaye asked, "It doesn't take that long to comb that hair of hers in a bun."

"Girl, finish your drink and relax, she'll be here." With that instruction, Kaye flopped down in the chair and drummed the glass with her nails.

"So how was Africa?" she asked.

"Hot and beautiful. Like me!" I giggled at my own joke.

"Well, I can't wait to see what happens with the whole bracelet thing that old woman gave you," she started, "that was kinda freaky, huh?"

"It was an experience," I admitted. "I will never forget it that's for sure."

Just then the doorbell rang. Kaye turned quickly in the direction of the door, glanced at her wristwatch and gulped down the rest of her drink. When I opened the door, my mouth gaped open and I stood aside to allow Vanessa to enter. She looked stunning.

"Look at you!" I gave her a hug and led her in. I patted her hair lightly. Kaye stumbled awkwardly out of her chair as she stood to greet Vanessa.

"Well look at Miss Thang!" Kaye hugged her just before Vanessa happily spun around like a ballerina while her shoulders were hunched.

"What do you guys think?" she asked us as she waited for a nod of approval.

"No bun," Kaye replied as she circled Vanessa, still clutching the empty glass. Her eyes were as big as golf balls as she smiled, obviously impressed with the transformation. Vanessa looked at me and winked knowing that she was ready to go out and dance the night away. "When did this happen?" Kaye was still checking out Vanessa's handy work.

"Well, I hadn't seen you guys in a while!" she confessed, "I felt I needed a change."

"Well, your hair and outfit look great," I told her. She had a shoulder length bob that was parted in the middle and slightly bumped on the crown of her head.

"Well alrighty then," Kaye said as she handed me her empty glass as if I were the maid, "let's go dazzle these fellas."

*   *   *   *

When we got to the club down by the water front, the walls were vibrating from the loud music as if it were an earthquake in progress that was sure to rip the building apart. The whole crowd on the dance floor looked like they were moving in unison to the go-go beat. Go-go and hand dancing was the big thing here in D.C. I had never even heard of go-go music or hand dancing until I moved here, and I'd lived in three states.

After Vanessa stood at the entrance taking in the scenery like a kid in Willie Wonka's Chocolate Factory, we bellied up to the bar and ordered some drinks. As soon as we found three barstools and adjusted our seats, this guy strolled up to Kaye.

"You want to dance?"

"I just got here. Maybe in a while," she smiled politely.

He looked at us, smiled and walked away. Kaye immediately erased the smile from her face, looked over at us and yelled, "Damn, can my butt warm the barstool first?"

I was unsure why Kaye was so offended. She knew that this was the usual drill. She typically was approached first whenever we went out dancing. Kaye, still perturbed, mumbled inaudibly before catching the attention of the bartender. Vanessa peered over at Kaye when she had to explain to the bartender the ingredients that made up the drink she had ordered.

Vanessa leaned in closer to me and said, "You guys aren't gonna abandon me are you? Just don't leave me alone. Don't."

She looked in my eyes with a frightened expression. Before I had a chance to respond, she looked around at all the club-goers, petrified of the mere thought of fending for herself.

"Girl, what's wrong with you?" I asked her. "We wouldn't do that. Loosen up, you are stiff! And stop looking like you've never seen people before. You know what? You need a drink. Let's order you one – and not the usual Virgin Mudslide."

I turned to the bartender ready to place my order. Vanessa politely tapped me on the shoulder. I turned to her and waited for her to say something, but she had her eyes focused at the end of the bar on a lady that just received her drink from the bartender. The lady took a sip and started coughing. The woman set the drink down, fanned her mouth as if it were on fire and clutched her throat.

"I don't want anything too strong, okay?" Vanessa cautioned me.

I sighed, shook my head, politely ignored her and ordered her a drink.

"She'll have a Liquid Cocaine and I'll have an Apple Martini."

Vanessa's face contorted to complete and utter bewilderment. "A Liquid Cocaine?" she asked, "What the heck kinda drink is that? No way, Hosea!"

"Trust me." I grinned and patted her on the back. "It will ensure instant fun."

The bartender handed us our drinks. I passed Vanessa hers and looked over at Kaye. Another guy was already in her face making small talk. I could tell that Kaye wasn't interested because she kept her eyes glued to the dance floor. Kaye didn't say a word to him even though she nodded her head every once and a while. When he told her to have a nice night was the only instance that she smiled and looked at him. I nudged her with my elbow to get her attention.

"You were rude . . . ," I said.

"Whatever," she sipped her drink, "you know I am not even thinking about hooking up with these men in here. Besides, his breath was sizzlin' the side of my face. Let's go over there." She pointed to an empty spot for the three of us that was close to the dance floor, but still next to the bar.

Kaye began to lead the way but we were stopped by another man after taking just a few steps from the bar.

No matter what event we go to, what outfit I'm wearing, if I'm tipsy or sober, I always and I do mean *always* attract the 40 something brother that thinks he is 25. This has historically been the type of man to first approach me whenever we have a girl's night out. It was as if this were some kind of test. He looked at Kaye and Vanessa and licked his chops, but I knew that I was going to be his victim.

"You are looking foxy fine tonight," he slurred and took a swig from an oversized bottle of Moet.

Kaye turned her head to laugh. Vanessa, who by now was feeling the effect of her drink, stared at him clueless as if he were speaking a foreign language and she was listening for an English word amongst his gibberish. My mouth had turned up in repulsion when I noticed him noticing me from across the room. Although being rude wasn't in my nature, I was about to be since I had become fed up with this prerequisite to a good time.

"Didn't foxy go out with the 70s?" I asked with an extremely dissatisfied smirk.

"You're still here, aren't you?" he said with a smile. His gold tooth shimmered under the strobe light. I could see Kaye's shoulders hunching up and down from laughing so hard.

"What do you want?" I asked, taking in his leopard print shirt. It was nestled underneath his bright yellow suit. Even this mofo's shoes and socks were yellow.

"Can I buy you a drink?" he sucked his teeth like he'd just finished eating a plate of pig's feet. I lifted my glass to indicate it wouldn't be necessary and forced a smile. He looked over the rims of his gazelles and apologized for not seeing the drink.

"Well, how 'bout a dance, lovely?"

"Actually, that's not a good idea, but thanks!" I turned my attention to the dance floor, an obvious cue for him to leave, but he didn't pick up on the hint. He just stood there looking at me up and down, grinning. I looked back at him perturbed and he turned to Vanessa.

"Is she always this mean?"

Vanessa shrugged, thought about his question briefly and then nodded.

"Well," he began, "don't you go too far 'hear? I wanna get a dance in with you before the night's done." He nodded while doing some two-step dance move that The Whispers would do, blew me a kiss, and then walked off like his Cash 5 numbers had just been announced.

"Girl!!!" Kaye turned around with tears streaming down her cheeks. "Why did you do your future ex-husband like that?"

Vanessa chuckled.

"I'm sick of it. What number was he Kaye, 20?" I took a huge gulp of my drink; it was time to get a little tipsy.

"20?" Vanessa asked, confused.

"Every time we go out, the first person to approach Sula is old, short and a wanna-be sugar daddy washed up player pimp." Kaye wiped her eyes, threw her head back and let out a hearty laugh. "I mean, every single time!"

Kaye had really enjoyed the little skit that Old Yeller performed because the broad was still laughing at my expense. About a full minute later, Vanessa joined Kaye and began laughing, finally understanding my rudeness and frustration. I took another huge gulp of my martini in hopes of muting out their raucous laughter. When it didn't, I turned away from them and faced the bartender. He pointed to me wondering if I wanted another drink, but I declined with the palm of my hand and continued swallowing down the one I had. I looked back at the bartender without being able to comprehend the blurred vision. Wobbling a bit as I gripped the edge of the bar to balance myself, I soon realized that the room was spinning. Just then, I felt a strong hand gently caress the small of my back. I ignored it and chalked it up to the alcohol consumption until I felt it again, but with more pressure. I turned around and refocused my vision.

Lawrence was standing in front of me with the hugest grin. My stomach felt like it was sinking and my mouth became dry at the same instance. He looked good and smelled better. He had on a grey ribbed mock turtleneck sweater with black slacks. That sweater of his accented his pectorals and biceps. He leaned in and gave me a kiss on the cheek.

"Hey, Sula!" He hugged me and I could feel his muscles contract when he squeezed. I'd almost forgotten how spellbinding his touch was. When he released me, he continued holding my hand. "Didn't expect to see you here."

"Yeah, it's girl's night out." I swayed in place as the alcohol and music moved me from side to side. I felt like dancing, but I wasn't about to dance with Lawrence. I reintroduced him to my girls instead. "You remember Kaye and Vanessa, right?"

Kaye looked him up and down and turned away. He smirked at her disrespectful gesture and then turned to greet Vanessa.

"Vanessa?? You look great!" He took both of her hands and held them away from her so he could get a good look at her frame. "Look at your hair! Love the shoes! Damn, you really look good, girl."

Vanessa smiled bashfully and patted her hair. "Thanks, Lawrence."

"Do you want to dance?"

Surprised at his question, I looked at Vanessa and waited for her response. His question took her off guard as well. She looked at me for approval. I shrugged and nodded.

"Go 'head, girl."

Lawrence led the way after Vanessa took his hand and followed him to the dance floor where they could prominently be seen by me and Kaye. Ignoring the urge to get jealous, I convinced myself that the point was for Vanessa to have a good time, not to get upset over Lawrence asking her to dance. Besides, he wasn't my man anymore. Kaye on the other hand didn't take it that way.

"What are you doing, ignorant?" Kaye always called people ignorant when they did or said something beyond her comprehension.

"What?"

"I know Lawrence is not trying to push up on Vanessa?"

"Kaye, they are just dancing."

"No, he is flirting. Look at him!" She pointed to the dance floor. Instead, I turned back toward the bartender, who pointed at my glass again to gesture for a refill. I shook my head as I held up the almost empty glass. Kaye spun me back around violently and aimed me in the direction of Lawrence and Vanessa.

Sure enough, Lawrence was flirting big time, and Vanessa was enjoying it. He whispered in her ear and smelled her hair. He even ran his fingers through it. He had his arms around her as they swayed back and forth. The music was fast, but they were slow dancing. He slid his hands slowly down her back, spreading his fingers wide to feel every inch. He went further down and I thought Vanessa would stop him, but he started palming her ass in front of everyone. She giggled and put her face in his chest as they continued dancing in their own world. I was a little perturbed, but what sense did it make to get bothered by a stupid dance from my silly ex?

"So what?" I told Kaye and turned back to the bar.

"So what??? Are you out of your mind? You better go over there and put a stop to that nonsense." She was motioning to the dance floor with her drink in their direction, spilling liquid on the floor.

"For what?"

She sighed heavily and looked back at them while shaking her head in disbelief. "For disrespecting you, that's what!" She slammed her glass down on the bar. The way Kaye carried on, you would've thought it was *her* ex that Vanessa was gyrating with and not mine.

"Kaye, I don't care. Lawrence is back at the airport in the unclaimed baggage section."

"Well, Vanessa should know better. You should at least be yanking her ass off that floor."

"Vanessa is here to have a nice time. I'm not gonna ruin her night over something I really *don't* care about, okay?" I swallowed the last sip of my drink and set the glass down.

It was time for me to have some fun and not worry myself with what Lawrence was doing. I was over him and he should know it by now. Kaye should have too, that's why I was a little surprised at how furious she had gotten.

"Relax, Kaye, it's not that serious. Let's go upstairs and see what's jumping up there." I said as I grabbed her arm while she stared at me as if she had something more to say. She stopped after a few steps and yanked her arm away from me slightly.

"You're gonna leave those two down here bumping and grinding all night long?"

Kaye loved drama, and the mere fact that I wasn't giving into it was turning her into a lunatic.

"Kaye, they are grown, they'll be alright, trust me. So are you trying to get your dance on or what?"

"I just hate it when you're calm! Alright, Sula. I'll let it alone."

"Thank you," I took her arm again as we started out of the crowded area, "now let's go." I glanced over at Lawrence and Vanessa one last time before ascending up the stairs. Maybe Vanessa was the one that he had been searching for, not me. I suppose that was my final test. I knew he was out of my system and this incident confirmed just that.

*   *   *   *

By the end of the night, Kaye had given her number out to three guys. I had given my number out twice, but they were fake. I tried to tell those two guys that I was not interested, but they wouldn't take no for an answer. I looked at my watch. Three o'clock. Kaye was finishing up a dance and I was sitting in this chair that felt like a huge cotton ball. My feet were killing me and I was beyond sleepy.

One guy that I had danced with a few songs earlier noticed how tired I was when I yawned in his face. I begged him to forgive me for doing that, but when I feel a yawn coming on, I can't hold it back. He said that it was okay, and then about five seconds later, he let one out himself. And it wasn't the quiet kind of yawn like mine was; it was the one where a loud "Haahhgg" comes out along with it.

My dancer chuckled with embarrassment and asked me to pardon him. I liked the fact that he had a sense of humor and was all about having fun. We danced for a good portion of the night and had a blast. When the

D.J. started playing some old school, we both dug into our repertoires and really started acting up. He snaked, while I cabbage patched and smurfed. He looked so funny when he broke out with the rooftop. I never thought seeing a tall lean guy do the rooftop could be so adorably comical. We both looked ridiculous, but we weren't the only ones showing out when Doug E. Fresh's "The Show" blared in our ears. I didn't offer him my number, but I took his.

His name is Ray Garrett and for the record, he is handsome. I had on heels, but we were almost eye-to-eye, so that made him about four inches taller than me. He had a dark, lean frame, which I could tell was muscular. He was bald and wore a tapered beard that framed his jaw line. His mustache framed his kissable lips and met up with his beard. He had bedroom eyes and his skin looked so edible in that cream colored shirt. I knew when he gave me his number that I would be calling him soon and very soon. I wasn't going to act pressed, but I was not about to let him forget who I was.

Vanessa and Lawrence strolled up to me while I was reminiscing about my encounter with Ray and making a mental note to put on my African bracelet before I went to bed that night. Ray had certainly gotten my attention. Vanessa's curls had fallen a bit and Lawrence's forehead was beaded with sweat.

"Well, look who didn't sit down all night!" I smiled at Vanessa and she returned a bashful smile before looking downward.

"Thanks so much, Sula. I had a great time."

"Well that was the plan."

"Are you and Kaye gonna be okay getting home?" she asked with a slight nod of her head.

"Yeah, why?"

"Lawrence offered to take me home if you don't mind."

I looked over at Lawrence and he looked down with a slight arrogant smile. He then looked on the dance floor at Kaye who was busy dancing, oblivious to everything and everyone.

"No, I don't mind," I looked at Lawrence with a bothersome expression. Vanessa grinned and latched onto Lawrence's arm. "Can I speak to you Lawrence? Vanessa can you excuse us?"

Lawrence looked in my direction with a smirk as if he had finally broken me down. Vanessa dropped her shoulders and backed away timidly.

"What are you doing, Lawrence?"

"What do you mean? I'm gonna give her a ride." He raised an eyebrow on the word "ride", at which I narrowed my eyes. "Are you jealous?" He rubbed his chin suavely.

"Please, okay? Jealousy is the last thing on my mind. I just don't want you to be screwing around with her emotions. She's always getting hurt by some guy."

"Why do you care?"

"Because she's one of my friends and I know how you are, Lawrence."

"Has it ever crossed your mind that I might be attracted to her and would like to have something meaningful with Vanessa?" He placed his hand on my shoulder.

"Lawrence, you don't fool me. If you're just doing this to get me upset, it won't work. You just *don't* mean anything to me anymore. So quit while you're ahead."

"You haven't lost your edge. I still like that." He winked and walked away. When he approached Vanessa, he put his arm around her and rubbed her shoulder. She turned and nervously looked back at me. I waved, forced a half smile and turned away. See, to Lawrence this was a game, but I thought what he was doing was a little too calculated for there to be a genuine attraction to Vanessa. Of course, she had finally come out of her shell, but why was he pushing up on one of my homies?

*   *   *   *

That night when I got home, I showered, took some aspirin and drank a full glass of water to stave off a nagging hangover the next day. I climbed into bed and slipped on the African bracelet. I took a deep breath as I latched it into place on my wrist and nestled myself under the covers. I was off to sleep in about five minutes.

I dreamt that I was in a wasteland. The trees were barren and grass was dry and brittle. It crunched beneath my feet as I walked. I wasn't sure where I was going, I just remember walking forward. The wasteland ran on to the horizon and seemed to never end. Slightly up ahead I saw a creek. The water looked murky, but there were two swans on the surface. They seemed oblivious to how murky the water was, that they were in the middle of nowhere, or that I was even present. When I got closer to the creek, a tall man who seemed to appear from thin air, stood beside me and took my hand. Just as I was about to look up and into his face to see who it was, the swans flew away and I immediately woke up.

I sat up in the bed and realized I had broken into a light sweat. I looked over at the digital read out on the alarm clock...5:16. *What was that about?* I thought to myself. I scribbled down the basic details of the dream on the notepad that I kept on the nightstand. Barren land, dry grass, murky creek, swans, tall man, hand holding. I tossed the pen and notepad back onto the nightstand and fell back on the pillow. Was that the guy that I just met or was it someone else, possibly Lawrence or someone from my past? I didn't want to stay up too long pondering over what the dream meant because I'd only had about an hour or so of sleep. I closed my eyes and tried to piece the dream back together. Forward and backwards, but could not figure out what it meant. Shortly thereafter, I drifted back off into a deep sleep.

Chapter Four - Lawrence's Secret

It had been a little over a week since I heard from Vanessa. The few times that I called, she wasn't at home, which was unlike her. I had supposed that the new Vanessa was finally doing a long overdue exploration of the city and its men.

Inspired by my trip from Africa, I was working on my first abstract painting, which was going to be based on the dream I had last night. I looked through an art book to get a feel of what other successful artists had done and was getting a bit frustrated. I was grateful that I had a vision of what I wanted to paint, but the problem was actually putting it on canvas. I wanted to capture it exactly as it was revealed to me in my mind. Just as I was about to wipe the canvas clean and start over, my phone rang.

"Hello?"

"Hey, what's going on?" Vanessa blared in my ear. Her voice sounded really alive and not as exhausted and uptight as it usually does. It was nice to hear this lively attitude for a change. Perhaps she wasn't spending that much time at work lately.

"Hey, girl!" I beamed. "I called you a few days ago. What's been up with you?"

"Oh, I've just been hanging out. How's it going, Sula?"

"Going good," I thumbed through my art book with the phone resting between my shoulder and ear. There was a brief silence between us although there was plenty of background noise on her end.

"So how's it going?" she asked – *again.*

I felt as though she was stalling, so rather than continue with the small talk, I rushed her. "Vanessa, what's up?" I asked flatly.

"Um, what are you doing now?"

"Nothing much, what's up?"

"Why don't you come and have a drink with me?" I couldn't make out the other voice in the background, but it was a guy.

"Hmm. Now? Where?" I asked suspiciously.

"I'm down in Adams Morgan, just hanging out."

I raised my eyebrows so far up I thought they were hovering over top of my head. She was drinking, on a weeknight? And hanging out in Adams Morgan? One sexy dress and she had become the social butterfly.

"That's not too far from me. Well, I guess. Give me about 20 minutes."

Vanessa told me that she was hanging out in this place called "Tryst". It was actually one of my old stomping grounds when I first moved to D.C. It was at one time my number one spot to just hang out and relax. It sort of reminded me of a big warehouse filled with flea market furniture. The only thing in the place that looked like it cost anything was the bar, which was probably left over from a previous restaurant before Tryst took up residence. Apparently, none of the customers seemed to mind the run down furniture; they were just there to have a good time with their friends and possibly make new ones. It was a shame I hadn't thought of this simple idea for a restaurant. The food was very inexpensive and they had things on the menu that you could easily make at home. Like a peanut butter and jelly sandwich.

When I entered, I looked around to see if I could spot Vanessa. Over the heads of several customers, I looked to the back of the restaurant as Vanessa shot up out of her seat and started waving maniacally like she was in the Macy's Day parade. I smiled when I recognized her because it felt like ages since I'd seen her. The hardwood floor creaked beneath my feet as I stepped toward her and noticed she had bought more clothes for the new her. She had on these tight assed jeans that looked spray painted on and a low cut poet's blouse that showed every inch of her cleavage. We met up about halfway, and her arms were extended to engulf me.

"Hey, Sula!"

"Hey 'Nessa girl, look at you! Don't hurt nobody!" It was all I could think of to say.

She took my arm and yanked me over to the couch where she had been sitting. My smile dissolved as I saw Lawrence sipping a beer while his lips were pursed into a wicked smile behind the rim of the bottle. He swallowed down the swig, looked up at me from his seat and gifted me with a one-sided grin.

"What's up, Sula?" he said, giving a single nod of his head while tilting the beer bottle in my direction.

"Lawrence . . ." I said through a heavy exhale, "what a surprise."

"It shouldn't be," he sat up, "I was sure Vanessa told you we have been hanging pretty hard lately."

"I didn't get around to doing that yet, Lawrence!" she sat me down and dumped herself between us creating a human wedge. As I scratched my head, I shook it from side to side with disbelief and confusion. Dancing together was one thing, but Vanessa was clearly giving me the brush off to hang out with my ex. I decided to *try* to have a nice time despite the awkwardness that they both created for me.

"I kind of figured you guys were, since that night at the club," I lied. I lifted my arm and frantically waved to signal the waiter.

"Yeah, Vanessa is a real party animal!" He put his arm around her waist and started tickling her. She giggled like a five-year-old kid watching Spongebob Squarepants.

"Lawrence!" she teased and playfully slapped his thigh.

The waiter didn't see me, so I stood up and signaled more vigorously. I was hoping I didn't look like Vanessa did when she was waving me over to her seat when I first walked in. After scoffing down what looked to be a mixed drink, the waiter came over. He was a young energetic guy, probably in undergrad studying law or something.

"What can I getcha?" He was overly chipper, but I didn't mirror his attitude.

"Give me a peanut butter and jelly sandwich," I said flatly as I handed him the menu, "and a cup of coffee. Black."

"Okie dokie." He sped off to place my order.

By the time I had placed my order and looked over at Lawrence and Vanessa, he was whispering in her ear and she was smiling and giggling so hard I thought her teeth were going to fall out. They were really making me feel like a third wheel and I didn't appreciate it. Honestly, I could've stayed at home and worked on my masterpiece, or gone somewhere else, than to sit here and deal with this foolishness.

"Vanessa, I'm gonna take a trip to the ladies room. Why don't you come with?"

"Oh, sure!"

"I thought you were a big girl, Sula?" Lawrence chimed in. "You need a chaperone for the toilet now?" He chuckled. This mofo was not about to have me acting ethnic in here, but I was getting tired of his stale performances – and for *who*? He was the one that let me go and supposedly couldn't live without my friendship, so why is he acting like I owe him something?

I gave him a quick evil eye, then smiled and said, "Just don't eat my peanut butter sandwich while I'm gone."

Lawrence smirked as if he didn't expect to hear that answer glide from my mouth with such ease and composure. He leaned back on the couch and spread both arms out relaxing them on the back of it. I thought to myself, *bastard*.

Vanessa and I made our way to the bathroom. This was hardly the place to have the conversation I was about to with Vanessa, but I had to know what was going on. When she realized I didn't have to go to the bathroom, she leaned against the sink with her arms folded and a concerned look on her face. I wasn't about to say a word until everyone left. I didn't want them going back to their table of friends pointing and saying, "See those two over there? That girl is seeing her ex-boyfriend!" I didn't feel like that kind of drama tonight. The last girl was finally done putting on her mascara, which changed nothing about her appearance. She fluffed her hair and left.

"What's wrong, Sula?"

"Vanessa, why did you call me to hang out with you and not tell me Lawrence was here?"

"It was his suggestion."

"Vanessa," I started, "I don't want to *see* Lawrence and it's bad enough seeing the two of you carry on like love sick high-schoolers."

"I thought you didn't care," she replied robotically as if she had been anticipating this discussion all week.

"Vanessa, turn it around, would you like it if I started hanging out with one of your ex-lovers and inviting you to spend time with *us*?"

"I just thought that when you said he could drive me home, that it was cool to hang out with him. I'm not trying to hurt you."

"It's not hurting me, Vanessa. If you choose to hang out with him, do it without me. You guys are making me feel like a third wheel out there."

"That's Lawrence!"

"It's both of you!" My loud voice resonated in the smelly and cramped ladies room. I took a deep breath and clasped my hands together as if I were about to pray. "Vanessa, I know how Lawrence is. He's trifling and doesn't care about anyone but himself. It seems as though he's trying desperately to make me jealous by using you. And you're allowing it."

"You think he's using me to make you jealous? Is that what you're saying?"

I shrugged and decided to let her make up her own mind. "Don't you think it's a little strange to have *you* call me down here when it was his suggestion?"

"Why can't he just want to be friends with me?" she said, as she turned her palms up, pleading with me to understand her side. "Now that I've decided to have some fun, you've got a problem with it."

"What? Me? Okay, Miss Fun, why Lawrence?"

"What do you want me to do, Sula?" She faced me, "Stop hanging out with him?"

I looked down. I was upset with myself for allowing Lawrence to spike a wedge between Vanessa and me. I was also peeved that I was even entertaining this ridiculous conversation with her. I placed my hands on her shoulders and looked her in the eyes.

"If you're having a good time with him, that's all that matters, right? I don't want to stand in your way." I walked out of the bathroom leaving Vanessa behind.

When I came back out to the dining area, Lawrence had this huge grin on his face. I ignored his idiocy and headed toward the front of the restaurant preparing to leave. He stood up and yelled my name. "Sula!"

I turned to face him, wondering what on earth he wanted from me at that point. He approached me stealthily and I backed up a few paces to protect my space. By now, Vanessa had made her way back to the bedraggled couch where we all were sitting.

"Where are you going?"

"Home."

"Now?"

"Yes. I don't know what kind of game you're playing, all I know is I don't want to be involved."

He chuckled and scratched his temple. "Game?"

"Uhhh yeah."

"You're the one playing the game, baby. Acting like us dancing together the other night didn't bother you. I know it did."

My mouth stretched wide to let out the loudest laugh as everyone in the restaurant faced me. "You have got to be kidding! I'm out." I turned and left.

After my heels dug into the sidewalk and started towards my car, I thought that I should've said more, but I had wasted enough breath on him. I was finally starting to understand what Lawrence's role had been in my life. He unequivocally enjoyed *trying* to hurt me. My task was to remain strong and overcome him. That was clearly someone that I didn't need in my life.

*   *   *   *

Kaye was beyond infuriated with the entire Lawrence-Vanessa situation and suggested that I cease speaking with both of them. After she vented, she suggested that we meet up after work to shoot a few games of pool.

Kaye picked me up from McPherson Square and we headed out to Alexandria. Once we arrived at the pool hall, she popped the trunk and I took out my cue stick and slammed the trunk closed. Kaye stepped out of her convertible, smoothed her hair back and put on a huge smile.

"Alright Sula, it's time to play dumb," she said.

"What?" I replied. "I know you aren't about to run some hustle."

She clicked the remote alarm on her keychain as we headed for the door and gave me a sassy smile.

"And I will take *all* of the chump's money. You know how I used to hustle in college."

"Yeah, I know. That's how you got most of your books and our food back then."

As soon as I opened the front door to the pool hall, the cigarette smoke and smell of old beer wrapped around us and invited us inside. I strolled up to the counter as if I were a professional player, and asked the manager to give us the best table in the joint. He chuckled at my silliness and shook his head. There were sounds of raucous laughter; some pop song playing on the jukebox and the sound of balls chiming sharply against one another on the green felt-topped tables.

"Table 20." He pointed toward the back of the hall and gave us a rack and a tray of balls.

"Okay, so how much are we playing for? $20 a game?" Kaye suggested.

"Hell, no! You're not hustling me! $1."

"A dollar??" She looked insulted. "Come on Big Cash, I know you have money, you just went to Africa. And I thought you've been practicing?"

"I have been practicing, but not every day! Big Cash? I'm still paying for that trip! How are you gonna hustle your friend anyway?"

"Alright, alright. We'll play a lousy buck a game," she threw her hands up in the air as if it were the most ridiculous idea in the world. "So did you find out what your man-swan dream meant?"

"No. I'm sure it will all make sense to me one of these days."

"Well, you know swans mate for life. Not sure what the murky, barren land thing means in contrast.

Maybe when things look bad you'll have a partner," she said with a shrug. I stopped in my tracks.

"Damn Kaye! You are brilliant! That makes perfect sense."

"Hey?" she turned and pointed the end of her cue case in my direction. "I'm not just gorgeous," she giggled. I fanned my hand at her silliness.

"But I wonder who is the guy?" I asked.

She continued walking and said over her shoulder, "You *need* to be praying that it was Idris Elba."

Table 20 was next to the rowdiest bunch in the hall. There were about five Spanish guys playing on one table and it was apparent that they had a few drinks. They missed several shots, kept bumping into each other as they passed one another, and giggled like young schoolgirls. As soon as we made our way to the table and the billiard light came on, they all stopped and stared in our direction.

Oh, lord, I thought, *if they keep staring, I'm gonna be nervous and lose a dollar to Kaye.*

"Hola." I heard a Spanish accent ring out.

Kaye and I looked over and said hello back. The few that I made eye contact with were handsome. At that point, I should've just handed my money over to Kaye.

"Damn, they kinda cute," Kaye whispered.

"Just rack 'em," I said.

After Kaye took several minutes racking the balls, I assembled my cue stick and chalked the tip. I could over hear the guys muttering something in Spanish. I knew a little bit and could make out the gist of the conversation.

In a nutshell, they thought Kaye and I were cute. They quieted down once we started our game. After I made the break and failed to sink anything, Kaye passed me when it was her turn.

"Girl, the one in the red shirt . . . mmphf."

I slyly glanced over. As soon as I looked, the guy with the red shirt was staring right at me. I tried to play it off with a smile and noticed that hey, he *was* fine. Kaye made her shot and missed. That's when the red shirt made his way over.

"Hey, how are you ladies doing?" He said with a thick accent. I could tell he was speaking slower than normal so we could understand him.

Kaye replied, "Just fine, you?"

She had totally taken her eyes off the table and locked with his. He was tall and had short curly hair and a wheat brown complexion. He had green eyes and a muscular build. Although he was among a good-looking bunch, he was by far the cutest of the group.

"Good good. Can I buy you ladies something for drink?"

I stood in the background with my chin resting on my hand that tented my cue stick. Kaye looked over at me. I nodded without raising my head. She looked back at him and nodded too. He beckoned the waitress over.

"Bring them whatever they'd like."

The waitress nodded, took our drink orders and walked off.

"So," he started, "Como te llamas? What's your name?"

"Kaye. You?"

"Manuel."

"Manuel. Hmm, that's my friend, Sula." Kaye pointed her cue stick in my direction.

"Sula. Very pretty name." He smiled and licked his lips.

I sighed deeply. I was wondering if Manuel knew exactly how fine he was. I waved and smiled. I didn't want to stare at him, so I decided to take a few shots while we waited for the waitress to return with my apple martini. I aimed for the nine to go into the corner pocket. Just when it was about to sink, one of Manuel's friends grabbed it. I looked up from my stance and followed the white v-neck sweater, past his broad shoulders, wide smile and up to the warmest most inviting dark honey colored eyes that I'd seen in real life. There were only a few people that I'd seen whose eyes smiled even when they weren't. He wore his hair in a fade that had huge dark waves on top. I stood upright and placed my hand on my hip, pretending to be agitated.

"Hey! The ball was about to go in."

"I know, but I wan' you to chute it again."

I was trying my hardest not to let the sound of his voice ripple down my spine, but I failed miserably. Even with his broken English, he had the most romantic accent that could've easily made Antonio Banderas sound like Porky Pig.

"Why?" I said. I smiled a little and watched as he approached me like a lion on the prowl.

"You were e-stan'in' all wron'."

"What was wrong with the way I was standing?"

He stood beside me and placed his hand on my waist and leaned me over slightly. He was mighty bold and I loved the feel of his hand on me. I looked over my shoulder into his hypnotic eyes, gladly allowing myself to be pulled into a trance-like state.

"You should be close to *la mesa* – the table. Hold your stick back here."

He took my hands and placed them on the back end of the cue. I could smell his cologne and took in a huge whiff.

"Okay, now what?" I said.

"All your power comes from back here. Watch the ball, with those *muy bonita ojos de sus*, pretty brown eyes of yours, aim and chute it again."

I sighed, tried to ignore his scent, his essence, and those eyes. Desperately I tried to erase the erotic shivers that toyed with my nerve endings when he touched me. I slowly looked in his direction and he was watching my form – or to be more specific, my ass. I aimed and shot. I raised myself up slowly as we both watched the ball's path. When the ball teetered back and forth from the hole and ricocheted from the rail, I gave him an unsatisfied smirk but tried to fight off a smile. He winked and smiled, then eased closer to me and looked at me up and down.

"You didn't listen to my instruction."

"Instruction?" I taunted, "I did and I missed."

He smiled, took my hand and placed his warm soft lips on the back of it. I looked at him and awaited an explanation. "Your name is Sula?"

"Yes."

"My name is Pedro."

There's something about when a Spanish man rolls his r's that entices me. He had a certain confidence about him that I found extremely attractive. When I glanced over at Kaye, she had totally forgotten about our game and was completely wrapped into Manuel. He couldn't take his eyes off of her. The waitress came back with our drinks. Pedro pulled out a bill and gave it to her. He handed me my martini, I gave a nod of thanks and then took a sip.

"You have pretty mouth."

"Thanks," I sighed at his highly *original* comment.

I set my drink down and prepared to take another shot, but he interrupted.

"You play me." He said and retreated to his table to grab his cue.

"You're not a sore loser are you?" I asked over the noise.

"What?" He turned his ear closer toward me as he headed back in my direction.

"You won't be upset when you lose will you?"

He laughed and turned to his friends and said something to them in Spanish. "*Esta mujer hermosa dice que Ella me batirá en un juego de la piscina.*" The crew chuckled lightly.

"You didn't have to tell them that I said I would beat you. I'm sure they heard me." I informed him with an intellectual smirk.

He raised his eyebrows and pouted his lower lip as his head nodded. "You know e-Spanish?"

"A little. Let's play," I purposely walked around him and brushed his back with my breasts just to mess with him. Pedro quickly racked the balls for a new game. Kaye was smiling like she was a contestant in the town beauty pageant as she enjoyed Manuel stroking her hair. I wondered if she noticed that he had on white socks. Being Kaye, I'm sure if she had, she would've said something by now. But from what I could tell, she hadn't taken her eyes off of his face every since he introduced himself. Neither had he. The other three guys in their group were almost done with their game and carried on as if we weren't even there.

"Every time I make shot, you kiss me," Pedro said matter-of-factly.

"I don't think so."

"Why no'?"

"I don't know you."

"I'm Pedro!" he smiled and made a shot. The ball sunk in the side pocket. He looked at me with his lips puckered awaiting a kiss. Even though I could've sucked his sexy lips right off of his gorgeous face, I fanned an uncaring hand as if the notion were a cloud of choking smoke. After that gesture, I told him to forget it. "Okay, okay. Maybe next time," he said.

"What makes you think there's gonna be a next time?"

"Because I wan' see you again."

He was definitely not the type to beat around the bush. For some strange reason after he said that, I thought about Ray and oddly felt like I was cheating. Although we hadn't gone on a date yet, we spoke quite a bit on the phone. I was unsure why I was experiencing this way too premature feeling of guilt. It was probably because I had found Pedro so attractive and he certainly was throwing some vibes in my direction.

"You say that to all the girls," I said, shaking that weird sensation of infidelity.

"All the other chicas are no' as pretty as you."

I huffed to myself when he wasn't looking and checked out his physique in between my agitation and intrigue. He scratched his three-day beard that was perfectly crafted on his face and grinned. His eyes invited me inside his soul as he pulled me in with his intoxicating stare.

"Whatever."

"Why you no believe me?"

"Because, I've heard it before. But without that sexy accent."

This time I made *him* blush and his adorable expression was coupled with a hint of embarrassment. He peered over at his friends who were all smiling, ribbing each other and chuckling. In an exaggerated smooth motion, I picked up my cue stick, twirled it behind my back and sank the seven into the side pocket. His buddies clapped for me as I basked in my great skill at billiards. As the clapping died down, I heard one staccato clap. I rose slowly as my smile faded and glanced over at

Pedro's friends who were all looking in the direction of the front door. Even Pedro turned to look. When I glanced over in Manuel and Kaye's direction, her face was grimly frozen. Manuel's small Adam's apple seesawed in his throat as he gulped hard. His widened eyes were fixated toward the front of the pool hall just over my shoulder. The sarcastic clapping ceased and I slowly turned to face the person that had rudely patronized me.

Lawrence.

He was becoming a plague. I'd entertained the idea of perhaps getting some sort of shot, or vaccine that could possibly rid him from my life forever. Was he stalking me? Why did he need to see and know everything that I was doing? At the club, it was a bit suspicious how he showed up not long after we had arrived. Then Vanessa told me that it was his idea to invite me to Tryst, not hers. Now, he was making an appearance at the pool hall less than 30 minutes of me and Kaye being there? I could feel the inner pit of my stomach rumbling like a volcanic eruption that would spew a violent stream of filthy expletives from my mouth. I slammed my cue stick on the table and folded my arms in front of me.

"Kaye? I'm ready to go," I stated firmly with my back toward her.

"No," she responded sharply.

I turned and looked at her as if she was being a defiant child and I was her mother. "I'm ready to go." I repeated more sternly.

"Don't let Lawrence run you outta here. Especially since you and Pedro were just getting well acquainted." She smirked at Lawrence and rolled her eyes.

Lawrence looked around at the scene he had just interrupted while I anticipated what excuse he'd come up with to explain his presence at this place. When he stared coldly at Kaye, I decided to break the awkward silence that had fallen across the back of the pool hall with a bit of sarcasm.

"So, is Vanessa here too?"

"I don't know. I don't really care either," he responded and then approached me.

My cue stick transformed into a samurai sword as I held it up in an attempt to keep him several paces away from me.

"What are you doing here, Lawrence?" I said as I waved the tip of the cue just under his nose.

"I'm not here for you, Sula," he said as he gently moved the cue out of his face.

In one sharp motion I flicked the cue to the base of his neck to show him I meant business. "Oh yeah? How do I know that?"

Pedro started giggling after I finished my question. He tried unsuccessfully to hold down his snickering that erupted into a sound of a flattened trumpet. As I glared at him with my eyebrows crumpled tightly together, he tried to straighten his face and wipe away his smile, but he just couldn't do it.

"Pedro? What's so funny?" I just had to ask.

Pedro shook his head and quieted down by clearing his throat a few times behind his smirk. I suspiciously eyed Lawrence.

"Okay, so what *are* you doing here?"I asked him.

"I was about to ask Manuel that same question."

At this point, I was totally confused.

"You know Lawrence?" Kaye asked as she looked at Manuel and sat at attention.

"Yes."

I looked around, confused by the whole ordeal, and surveyed the room for everyone else's reaction. There were looks of indifference, one of cynicism, grief, and total bewilderment.

"Pedro, what's going on here?" I asked him, motioning to Lawrence and Manuel.

"Let me get you another drink," Pedro distracted.

"No, I'd like to know what's going on." I turned to address Lawrence, "Lawrence?"

"Shut up, Sula," Lawrence responded as he raised his hand in a silencing motion and avoided eye contact with me.

Manuel put a consoling and calming hand on Kaye's shoulder. "Kaye? Go wait for me outside," he instructed.

"For Lawrence? No way!"

"Kaye, *por favor*, please."

"Alright, alright, I'll be outside. Come on, Sula." Kaye reluctantly stood up and grumbled the entire time from when we walked out of the pool hall to the parking lot.

"I'm sick of your ex!!"

"You? How do you think I feel? I can't believe he told me to shut up."

"What is his problem? I know he didn't just interrupt a conversation I was having with that fine assed man in there!" She jumped up and down in a tantrum.

"Kaye, calm down. He told you to wait for him. Maybe they've got some business to take care of or something."

"What are you talkin', girl? He busted in there like he was Dolemite or somebody."

"What do you want me to say, Kaye? Go back in there and beat Lawrence with two cue sticks?" I offered. I nervously chuckled as Kaye stared at me blankly.

I mirrored Kaye's sentiments because I was just as baffled as she. Kaye opened her car door and threw her purse inside. After she slammed the door, she leaned roughly on the side of the car and looked down at her watch.

"He's got five minutes. After that, I'm leaving."

Just as she said that, Pedro walked outside with his arms outstretched, wearing a heavenly smile. He looked around the parking lot, taking in the scenery and strolled over to me and Kaye.

"Pedro," I started, "what's going on? Do you know Lawrence?"

"No, I only see him a few times."

"Where is Manuel?" Kaye said, overlapping Pedro's words and peering toward the entrance.

"He still inside. He say to give you this," Pedro handed Kaye a card.

"Why couldn't he come out here and give me the number himself?" She looked at the card and handed it back to Pedro.

Pedro didn't except the card and left Kaye extending it to him. "He's talking and talking, and said it will take a while to be done. He say to call him."

Kaye dropped the card to the ground and hopped inside the car. She slammed the door shut, turned the radio volume to about 50, and then put the top up on her car. Although the top was now up as well as the windows, Pedro and I could still hear the bass from the hip hop music. I flashed Kaye a quick, scornful look in hopes that she wouldn't think for a second that I wanted to hear that loud music all the way home. Pedro picked up the card and handed it to me.

"See that she gets this."

"Sure." I took it and slipped it into my purse. Pedro pulled out another card and placed it in my hand.

"Here is all my numbers. Call me."

"Can I ask something?"

"Anything."

"You guys don't deal drugs do you?" I strained my eyes as I tried to read his reaction. He laughed loud and hard at the very idea.

"No, sweetheart. I don't even know that guy! I talk to you soon." He gave me a kiss on the cheek, tapped my chin and strolled away just as smoothly as he had made his way over. Everyone was being overly secretive. I didn't understand what the big deal was, but I was about to find out. It had to have been something extremely big for everyone to be so tight-lipped. Lawrence had sounded as if he and Vanessa weren't hanging out anymore, which seemed mysterious since the other day they were all over each other in Tryst. I opened the passenger side door as the music's volume got louder and decided that I was going to call Vanessa once I got home.

"You have to turn that down!" I yelled over the music.

Kaye turned it down and backed out of the parking space violently.

"Hey, you're not gonna kill us, just because the guy didn't come out and give you his number personally are you?"

"Maybe. And why did he have his boy hand me his number? What was up with that? And then stopped our conversation because Lawrence walked in? You would've thought Lawrence was a detective or something. Naa, something don't seem right and that's why I left that number right on the ground where it belonged. I don't do that shady stuff, Sula. You know that." She skidded into a right turn. My head jerked with the movement of the car and I glared over at her.

"I know you're a little upset . . ."

"A little??" She threw on her left signal and veered wildly into the left lane. "I'm damned bent outta shape over here."

"Okay, I know you're bent out of shape, but calm down. My ass cheeks are about to rip the leather right from this bucket seat! You're driving like a maniac!" Kaye lowered her speed limit and sighed. "Now I'm sure if you just call Manuel, he'll give you an explanation. If he didn't care, he wouldn't have offered his number at all." I slipped his card into her purse.

I pulled down the visor to check my lipstick which still seemed intact. Fishing around in my purse, I found a pack of gum and offered Kaye a piece which she declined. She was upset alright. She never turned down gum.

"You know what? Let's go check on Vanessa. She may actually have some scoop. I told you about her and Lawrence at the restaurant the other day, right?"

"Yeah, trifling asses," she muttered.

"Well, for him to say that he didn't know where she was and didn't care, something must've gone down. I say we go get the 411."

"Sula, can I ask you something?" Kaye turned to look at me briefly when we reached the stoplight.

"Yeah. What is it?"

"How do you stay so calm and collected?" She awaited my answer. "I just know if Vanessa had been hanging with one of my ex's, I would've pimp slapped her. Three times. Then I would've kicked her when she was down on the ground! And you didn't get the least bit offended when Lawrence showed up, or when you saw those two together the other day. What's up with that?"

"I don't know how to explain it, Kaye. That trip to Africa opened my eyes to a lot of things. The bottom line: there was really nothing I could do in either of those situations, so why get an ulcer over it?" I stared out the window to see a group of youngsters loitering in front of a doughnut shop. I looked straight ahead at the road before us. "To tell you the truth, I think Lawrence has some mental issues. It actually scared me when he showed up. He was the last person I'd thought I'd see tonight. What if he's stalking me? And rather than make him upset and have him flip out, I'd prefer to just keep my distance."

"Well, you can't keep your distance if he keeps showing up everywhere you are."

"True, but what can I do?"

"Get yourself a nickel plated .38."

I laughed, "Okay, now you are really scaring me. First you speed outta the parking lot like Vin Diesel, now you going vigilante like the old dude in the movie Taken? Do you need a hug?"

She laughed and shook her head. "No girl. I've just never seen you cut loose on anyone. You're always sophisticated. I think that's cool though, Sula."

"Well thank you, girl. And trust me, it's not easy to do all the time."

We pulled up in front of Vanessa's three-story townhouse out in downtown Silver Spring. Her lights were on, so we figured she was at home.

"What if there is a man in there with her?" I inquired.

"Yeah, right."

Kaye unfastened her seatbelt. Before we got out of the car to drop by Vanessa's unannounced, I gave Kaye a brief speech. It was as if I were being a mother that lays out the ground rules for behavior before entering a store with outrageous children.

"Okay, let me do the talking and don't get all upset over the fact that her and Lawrence were hanging out with each other. We're here to find out some facts. Got it?"

Kaye took a long pause and looked me up and down disgustedly. "Girl, get your ass outta my car and ring that doorbell."

I took that to mean she understood where I was coming from.

We stood on Vanessa's porch. The sound from her television could've shattered her windows. It sounded like a war was occurring behind her storm door. I flashed a concerned look to Kaye who imitated my sentiment. I rang the bell twice in case Vanessa couldn't hear it. We heard the TV's volume decrease and then her footsteps. She peered out of her sheer curtain and opened the door.

"Hey. What brings you ladies by?" She smiled as she opened the door wide enough for us to enter. I entered and immediately looked on her TV screen to see what she was watching. It was an old western film and everyone was getting shot, beat up or falling off of a horse. Then I looked at her coffee table. I hadn't seen that much junk food since the last time I went into a convenience store.

"Hey girl . . ." I said nervously. "What you doing?"

"Watching westerns and stuffing my face." She laughed and sat down.

"Why are you eating all of this junk food? I thought you were trying to keep your weight down?" I looked at the array of snacks that were blanketing the table. There was a half-eaten sub, Buffalo wings, a huge container of grape soda, chips, dip, Hershey's kisses and some carrot sticks.

"Just binging. It's been so long since I had any of this kind of food. I got a little bored with the cans of tuna, salad and liter bottles of water, ya know?" she explained while popping another Dorito in her mouth and crunching down on it. "Sit down, sit down."

Kaye and I took a seat on the couch. Vanessa took her seat back on this huge throw pillow she'd had on the floor in front of the coffee table and the food. "What brings y'all by? I haven't talked to you guys in a while."

"Yeah, I kinda figured you were busy with Lawrence, that's why I've been a little silent on my end." I said, trying to feel her out on the subject. I darted my eyes quickly to Kaye and she gave an affirming nod.

"Oh, Lawrence," she scoffed. "Whatever!"

"What happened, Vanessa?" Kaye asked, as she grabbed a few carrot sticks and Hershey's kisses.

"Lawrence is very confused. He doesn't know what he wants out of life."

"How do you mean?" I asked. I reached over and grabbed a few chips.

"Well, he just kind of pushed me out of his life. I mean, things were going pretty good and then he just stopped calling. I called him and he didn't return any of my calls. I didn't understand. I didn't do anything to him to deserve that. Then for a second, I thought he'd gotten back together with you, Sula."

"Me? Why'd you think that?"

"He talked about you a lot and how much he messed up."

"Yeah, he did mess up," Kaye offered as she crunched down loudly on a carrot stick.

"Anyway," Vanessa finished, "he said he didn't think he was cut out for dating anymore – that he wanted to try something new. I *thought* he meant me. But after the conversation you and I had in the bathroom that day, I had already made up my mind that I wouldn't do that."

She took a huge bite of her sub and continued speaking with her mouth full and words distorted.

"So one night, I see him in the mall parking lot," she said with a hint of suspense in her voice.

I was sitting on the edge of the couch by this time. I knew coming here would answer the questions both Kaye and I had about tonight's strange turn of events.

"He was with some Spanish guy. It looked like they were arguing. He tried to hug the guy, but the Spanish guy kind of pushed him off. So Lawrence sort of stepped away and the guy reached for him, and BAM!"

"He hit his ass?" Kaye asked with widened eyes as she anxiously awaited the conclusion.

"No! The Spanish guy planted a juicy one on Lawrence. Right on the lips!"

Both Kaye and I gasped. I placed my hand over my mouth after doing so. Kaye dropped a few of her carrot sticks on the floor. The Spanish guy had to have been

Manuel. It was too much of a coincidence. For some odd reason, I imagined Lawrence and Manuel in a passionate exaggerated embrace, tongues intertwined, heavy panting and groping. I cringed at the mere vision. Not because it was two men, but because one of the men I'd been with intimately!

"Holy crap," Kaye said.

Vanessa shook her head and gulped down a swig of soda. I couldn't believe my ears and I guessed neither could Kaye. She was into the western film until Vanessa said "right on the lips".

"Oh no," was all I could manage in a hushed tone.

"Wait. This Spanish dude, was he tall and real fine?" Kaye asked quickly.

"Yeah," Vanessa confessed while nodding rapidly. "*Real* fine. I thought he was just doing that to get rid of me for good, but *he* didn't know I'd be at the mall. I started to get out of the car and approach him, but didn't see the point."

"Naa, you just stayed in the car and continued to be nosey!" Kaye noted. Vanessa laughed and nodded her head while she took another large bite of her sub.

"I called him the next day and told him I saw him at the mall," Vanessa started. "He opened up to me like I was Oprah. Come to find out, the Spanish guy, Manuel, was an old friend of his who'd come back into town. So I asked Lawrence how long did he know he was bisexual. Without hesitating, he said all his life. I told him that it didn't matter what or who he preferred, that I'd still be his friend. But, that was kinda it. I haven't heard from him since then."

"All his life . . .?" I quietly asked myself.

"Yep. All his life."

I stood up almost in slow motion and made my way to Vanessa's kitchen. I overheard Kaye yell out, "I knew that mofo *had* to be gay! Wearing them tight clothes!" I reached up to get a glass from Vanessa's cabinet. I poured myself a glass of water to rid the Dorito taste from my pallet when it hit me.

He broke up with me because he wanted to see other people. He wanted to see men! More specifically, Manuel. I set the glass down on the counter and shook my head back and forth several times in disbelief. That's worse than him leaving me for another woman, or is it? This explains a lot about his erratic behavior, occasional disappearances and constantly wanting to hang out in Dupont Circle. Thank God for condoms!

I thought about all of the anguish he'd subjected me to because he wanted to be with another man. I struggled to maintain my balance because the news made my legs feel as firm as Jell-o. I staggered back into the living room to rejoin the girls. Vanessa eyed my every move. She brandished a smirk across her lips before she spoke.

"Sula, I know what you're thinking. That he broke up with you to be with a man. I thought the same thing too. But Lawrence is one confused individual. Now, there's nothing wrong with same sex relationships, I just don't think he should've been with you that long knowing he was bisexual and now gay. Don't blame yourself," she finalized her speech with stifled laughter.

"I don't blame myself," I said, clearing up any confusion Vanessa may have had. "I mean, I won't lie, it's insulting as hell, but it wasn't my fault. He summed it up when we broke up. It was him, not me."

*   *   *   *

When I returned home and prepared for bed, I thought about the entire Lawrence/Manuel situation. Before I invested too much of my thoughts on the matter, I remembered that I met Pedro and we both were interested in one another. I reached for the African bracelet and put it on my wrist. I wrote a bit in my journal and then turned over once I had begun to get sleepy. I drifted off to sleep and once again, my subconscious took over.

I dreamt that I was at an amusement park. The park was unoccupied, but the rides were fully functional and operating although there were no passengers on them. Bells and whistles were blaring at almost each turn. Not a soul was in sight. I remember having an overwhelming sense of anxiety. I almost felt as if I were hyperventilating. I just wanted to leave the park. The smell of stale donuts and dried cotton candy turned my stomach. The stench seemed to follow until I found the park exit. Sand covered the cracked asphalt, while some featured rides were missing colorful bulbs from its flickering title. When I finally found the park exit to prepare to leave, there was a man standing there. I couldn't see his face, but he wore a dingy gray robe that was frayed at the hem. As I walked by, the man stopped me. I redirected my steps to go around him, but he hindered my exit again. I turned to walk back into the park just to get away from the strange man. To no avail, I quickened my pace and he followed me. The air seemed to get thinner as I started to run toward the house of mirrors. I wanted to see the face of the person who was following me. Just as I was about to enter the mirrored rooms of confusion, the man's hand gripped my shoulder. I turned to see who was restraining my escape. Just as I turned, I woke up.

I sat up in the bed and breathed in and out frantically. I looked around my bedroom although my eyesight had not adjusted to the darkness. Even though I was alone, I had the strange feeling that someone was in the room with me, but I knew that was not possible. I reached for my notepad and jotted down the vital details of the dream. Amusement park, exiting, mirrors, a man, feeling trapped. Again, I was confused and wondered what it all meant. Perhaps it would all be revealed to me soon.

Chapter Five - Busted

Sipping my ice cold ginger ale, I tried my best not to stare into his big dark eyes. I was glad we had the chance to see each other again under natural light instead of those club lights. Right away, I could tell that Ray was intelligent and sophisticated, but down to earth. He could make me laugh so hard, which I really adored about him. These were characteristics that I found extremely attractive. He and I had spoken by phone almost every night since we met. I was really beginning to like him, but I didn't want to get ahead of myself. Not to mention that I didn't know what that dream meant after I met him, or even if it were reflective of he and I. I was certain that the more that we talked the more I liked him. Even though we chatted by phone, it had been a few weeks since we saw each other. Our schedules just didn't seem to link up until now.

Secretly, I studied every inch of his being as he sat across from me and made small talk. When he reached for his glass, I looked at his hands and imagined how exquisite it would feel to have them wrapped around my body; rubbing and teasing my mounds and crevices. I wanted this man.

"How's your food?" I asked him.

"Not too bad, sweetheart," he said with a satisfying sigh.

"Yeah, that's not too bad, but I make a pretty good salmon too!" I said confidently as I flaked off another piece.

"You don't know how to cook!" he teased. "For real? You sure you know how to cook?" He squinted his eyes and gave me a suspicious frown.

"Yeah, man. I can cook anything." I gave a reaffirming nod.

"Really?" he rubbed his chin and then asked with a Jamaican accent, "Anyting mon?"

I giggled and said, "Ya mon! It's irie."

"Can you make sautéed buffalo toes with buzzard beak stew?" Somehow he managed to get it out with a straight face.

I, on the other hand, gagged on my drink as I tried to contain my laughter. I reached over and grabbed the linen napkin from a nearby place setting and covered my mouth to keep the liquid from oozing from my nose and mouth.

"That's a delicacy in some nations. You have to really know how to get the toe jam out of those buffalo hooves. You can't just soak 'em in Epsom salts, you gotta get up in there! I won't even get started on the buzzard beak. You gotta scrape the roof of their mouth out with a special paste," he let out a tiny snicker as he awaited my answer, which made me want to laugh even more.

"You know what? You are so silly, Ray!" I said as I tried to compose myself from the joke. Ray was fine. Even though he could be silly, which pleases me, he had been a complete gentleman – in the restaurant and on the phone. So far so good.

"I like to clown around, so don't mind me," he said, "Okay, let me get serious. So Sula, how's the art business?" he asked.

"It's doing really great. We're having an exhibit in a few weeks."

"Who's the featured artist?"

"Oh there are three. Michael McBride, Sam Odoi and Brenda Joysmith," I said smoothly. "Mr. McBride has this oil painting I want called 'Metamorphosis'. Inspirational! His work has even been featured on Living Single, the Jamie Foxx Show and I think Soul Food. He has to sign it for me though. There will be a lot of upscale folks there. The mayor is coming."

"Really?" he sounded surprised and interested as he sat back in his chair with his brows raised. "Speaking of the series of Soul Food, you sorta look like the girl who played Teri," he noted.

"Yeah, I get that a lot."

"Not exactly, but very similar. You're beautiful, Sula. Those eyes."

"Well, thank you."

"So it sounds like your art exhibit will bring in some good exposure for your gallery. Among it being a great networking opportunity. A lot of folks will be there. You know I've always enjoyed the arts," he said with a nod. I guess that was my cue to invite him, so after a dramatic pause, I did.

"Would you like to be my escort?"

"Hell, I'd love to be your escort."

"You *do* have a tux, don't you?"

"Of course," he replied without hesitation.

That turned me on even more. Something about a man owning his own tuxedo meant to me that he took his appearance seriously, was prepared for any formal event, and that he had gone to a few black tie events before and had some etiquette. He had probably been around some very influential people as well. It was time to find out some more information about this hunk. So far, our whole conversation had been about me.

"So tell me about your job," I inquired. "Well, you don't have a job, you have a career. It sounds exciting!" I boomed.

He smiled, wiped his mouth with his napkin and took a labored deep breath. I crinkled my eyebrows, but still smiled, wondering what all the anxiety surrounding his profession was for. "It actually is exciting, but it's a lot of work. A lot of traveling. Do you like to travel?"

"I sure do. I just came from Africa last month," I informed him.

"Oh wow. Yes, I've been there. I love that restaurant Carnivore," he told me.

I became instantly attracted because we had something else in common. "Isn't Carnivore great? I can't believe I ate a zebra."

"Tastes like chicken!" We shared a laugh. "Well, my career doesn't require me to go to Africa, but I go all over the U.S."

"Ray, what made you want to be a sports agent?"

"I love sports, babe. I can't lie, I'm a man. But I'm a man of vision. Instead of just sitting there watching boys and grown men play and get hurt, I was curious. When I was in junior high school I wondered how those guys got selected to play. To be on t.v., you know? So I started researching and decided that was what I was going to do. I wanted to be the guy who put them on t.v."

"Well, it's not every day I meet someone who's a sports agent. It seems like it could be fun and have a lot of rewards," I replied.

"Yes, as a matter of fact, it is. I'm on the road a lot, doing meet and greets. Free tickets. I enjoy it, but it could be hard at times too." His eyelids dropped lower as he stared out into nowhere. "So, um…you know, that's why I'm single. No one can handle the schedule. I need a strong independent woman who I can trust and who trusts me. Like someone who owns her own art gallery…" he smiled at me and fiddled around some more with his salmon. I just smiled at the hint he dropped. He certainly knew what to say and when.

"Let's see how you look in that tux first," I playfully teased him.

He gave me a sexy smile and nodded before he said, "I really like you, Sula. We're going to have so much fun together."

*   *   *   *

I walked down to the kitchen of the Marriott to make sure that the caterer didn't need any last minute items before preparing to put the hors d'oeurves out for the guests. She assured me that she had everything under control and would be ready for the guest's arrival at 7 p.m. when the doors opened. She complimented me on my wine colored charmeuse floor length halter gown. I was receiving compliments all night from the hotel staff as well as my own staff. I had pinned my hair up in a dry French roll and had a sweeping bang. The only things that were missing were the glass slippers. The day before, I'd spoken to all of the artists who couldn't wait to showcase their work. So far, everything was going according to schedule. However, I was beginning to get butterflies in my stomach because I would be seeing Ray again – this time in a formal setting. It would be the first time in a little over a week.

I ran through my mental checklist of items to make sure I hadn't left any stones unturned. I stood in the middle of the room where I'd be introducing the artists and my eyes darted around to check that all items were intact. As I stood there, I murmured to myself and used the tips of my fingers to double check that last minute issues were closed.

My assistants, Gayle and Tara, propped the doors open at 6:30 and people were already beginning to arrive. I walked briskly over to them to give some last minute instructions.

"The guests can hover in the lobby. Make sure they don't try to go into the exhibit halls though. I'm doing a last minute run through," I instructed.

"Okay," they both said in unison.

As I prepared to walk away, I heard someone from outside call my name. "Sula? Miss Sula Tyler?"

I turned toward the direction of the voice. Ray had stepped forward past the small crowd of people and an instant smile came to my lips when I saw him. He looked great at the club, edible at lunch the other day, but tonight, he looked a zillion times better. That old saying went, "clothes make the man," apparently, whoever coined that cliché didn't see Ray. It was obvious that he was making that tuxedo.

"Wow look at how handsome you look," I said.

"No! Look at you. You look absolutely stunning." He took my hand and kissed the back of it. Then he pulled me closer and kissed me on the cheek. He was so gallant.

"Why thank you. Why don't you come on in? I was just doing a last minute walk through. Join me?" I locked my arm with his and led the way.

"I'd follow you anywhere, with your fine self," he said with a warm smile. He stepped in and greeted Gayle and Tara with a wave and a nod. They both stared at him as he entered with their mouths slightly gaped. I smiled at their reaction to Ray and motioned jokingly for them to get back to work by fanning my hands in a scooting motion. In response to my silent instruction, those silly girls gave me the "thumbs up" and the "okay" sign.

"This is beautiful," he said looking up and around. "But it doesn't compare to you. You are gorgeous, baby. Dare I say you look good enough to eat?"

He smiled his pearly toothed, one dimpled smile. I could tell that he just had his goatee and beard shaped up. He didn't drown himself in his cologne, rather he seemed skilled enough to let the aroma flirt with my senses, not overpower them.

"Oh yes," I responded cheerfully. We took a stroll to another meeting area just before the exit to the terrace. The five-string quintet was warming up and took a break to greet us. "You guys aren't nervous are you?" I joked. They guffawed and replied with scattered "no's."

"You're so charismatic," Ray said without the complementary smile, which added to the validity of his statement. "So will the patrons be able to purchase artwork on the spot?"

"At some of my events, I allow it. But I decided against it for this one. I wanted to do custom orders. The goal is to have the patrons stay and discuss their selections with the artists and myself. I want to sell the total package, the print, matte and the framing. It's a win-win situation for me and the artist. Hosting these galas is the best part of my job."

Just as I finished my statement, Ray pulled me toward him and planted a soft seductive kiss on my lips. I could feel his fingers spread wide as he pressed his body into mine. While his hand moved down the small of my back, the other held my hand loosely by my side. After the kiss, he slowly and gently pulled his body away from mine and gazed into my eyes. I pressed my lips softly together to redistribute my lipstick.

"Not that I'm upset, but what was that for?" I said, smoothing my hair in place as I displayed a babyish grin.

"For inviting me. I couldn't wait to see you again. I appreciate that sweetheart."

"Okay, Ray, you've already gotten major brownie points for showing up looking as good as you do. You don't have to try too much harder," I giggled.

He firmly gripped my hand, "It's true. I had a good time with you when we went to lunch and you've been on my mind every day since then. I've got to fly out to Sacramento tomorrow. But once the season is over, I'll have some down time and I'm definitely trying to fill up your calendar."

I smiled and placed my hand over his. "That's a plan. Honestly, I've thought about you too."

For the rest of the night, I'd be thinking about his soft warm kiss too. I glanced at the grandfather clock that read six-forty.

"Uh oh, one second," I told Ray while I poked my head through the terrace doors. I told the quintet to get started because I was about to let the guests in. They nodded and began playing a classical tune by Mozart.

"Time to work?" Ray asked.

"Yes, but don't go too far. We're gonna finish this conversation."

He threw on an old Southern accent and pointed both fingers at me, "I'll be right c'here waitin'." He grinned and winked. I had almost forgotten how silly he could act with his fine self.

"You are too crazy!" I scurried off to the entrance while he watched.

The guests had already started mingling in the large marble foyer. They hovered over the hors d'oeurves and collected glasses of champagne from the bartender. Several congressmen, senators and council members had arrived – and of course, the Mayor. I had also invited art collectors from my database to peruse the inventory for tonight. This was an event that was sure to make each of the three artist's careers more stable after tonight and everything had to be perfect.

I saw Ray make his way into the main foyer as he began to mingle. I thought this was impressive. He didn't feel uncomfortable in this setting and wasn't fusing himself to my side. I glanced over and watched him as he made light banter with the guests. He was charming and did I mention fine in that tuxedo?

I sauntered over to Gayle and Tara. "How are you ladies holding up?"

"Ummm, my corns are *simmering*," Tara said jokingly, but with an edge of seriousness.

"Just dip those dogs in some boiling water when you get home. For now, try not to think about the pain.

How are you, Gayle?" I rubbed my hands together nervously.

"Fine, but I just need to know . . . who was the hunk that came in earlier?"

"Hunk? Haven't heard that in a while. Umm, he's a friend of mine," I grinned proudly. "His name is Ray."

"Yes well, does Ray have any brothers?" Gayle asked.

"Hmm, I don't think so."

"Uncles? Cousins? Widowed father?"

*   *   *   *

I made my way to the center of the foyer to announce the artist's presentations. The time had finally come for them to open their exhibits to their potential buyers.

"Ladies and gentlemen, may I have your attention, please?"

Everyone quieted down and looked in my direction. I spotted Ray who wore a grin that spanned from here to Atlantic City. There was still no sign of Kaye and Vanessa. Those two were almost an hour late.

"Good evening. I'm Ms. Sula Tyler and I'd like to take this time to welcome you to my third annual New Artist Showcase with Tyler Fine Art and Gallery. This special event showcases three superior artists this year. We have Sam Odoi," I motioned where his hall would be as he stood in front with his scissors ready. He waved to the crowd as they applauded. "Michael McBride." The audience applauded again. I heard a few whistles in the distance; maybe they were his family and friends. "And

Brenda Joysmith." The crowd clapped again. "Remember, you can also place custom orders with the gallery this evening and for tonight only they will be discounted at a hefty 30 percent."

The crowd responded with impressive murmurs when they were informed of the discount.

"Thank you for taking time out to join us this evening. So if you haven't done so, grab some pâté, a glass of wine, and then hurry on over to see what these brilliant artists have recreated on canvas from their hopes, dreams and fulgent imaginations. Artists? You may now unveil your dramatic works!" The crowd applauded yet again.

Almost simultaneously, each artist cut their ribbons that once banned entry to the exhibit area. The crowd slowly sifted into the three different halls. However, Ray made his way over to me as he gently clapped his hands together and smiled.

"Marry me," he said as he took my hand. I giggled at his sentiment. "You don't understand how much of a turn on it is to see a woman that has her stuff together, can articulate her thoughts to a crowd of people, and help other African-Americans who are trying to make it. Damn. And you fine too, girl."

"Thank you, but I thought that was the whole point?" I chuckled again.

"Not to rush, but you wanna get some dessert and coffee afterwards?"

"That sounds good. My girls mentioned a jazz spot afterward. Those heifers. They are late! Let's play it by ear. We can ditch them if you'd like," I giggled at the comment.

"That's cool too. Okay, I'm gonna take a look at the artwork, but I'll be back out in a few. Okay, baby?" he asked.

"Sure, go right ahead. Let me know if you see something you like."

"I already do," he said as he stared at me up and down. He slowly backed away with his arms out by his side as he smiled. He clasped his hands and took one last look, then turned to walk into Sam Odoi's exhibit hall.

Damn, I thought. He was turning out to be quite the escort. I walked over to Gayle and Tara, they were chit chatting and giggling.

"Why don't you two grab a bite and have a seat? Give those corns a rest. After this event is over I have something for you both at my car."

"Okay," they said in unison again.

Just as they walked away, I saw Kaye and Vanessa heading up the walkway along with three other people. One of them went back to the car as the others strolled up to me. They looked great; no wonder they took such a long time.

Kaye had on a long, fitting satin dark purple strapless gown with a matching sheer stole draping her arms. Her hair was pinned in a French roll, but she had these huge spiral curls cascading her face. Vanessa wore a black velvet sweetheart cocktail dress. What really made the dress was that it had three thin silver chains that linked the velvet choker to the front of the dress. The dress was gorgeous and Vanessa looked fantastic in it. She wore her hair the same as she had when we went to the club.

"What took you heathens so long?" I asked, giving them both hugs.

"Believe it or not, it was Vanessa! She had to make sure none of those damned chains were twisted! You look good, girl!" Kaye said as she inspected my gown. "Anyway, let me introduce you to my date, Scott. He's a personal trainer. Scott this is my bestie, Sula."

I shook his hand. He was a bit shorter than Kaye and very muscular. He looked like a pint-sized Michael Clark Duncan, the big guy that played in the movie *The Green Mile*. His arms were so huge they looked like cannons that set out about six inches from his sides. Even his face was muscular. I hoped my expression remained hidden, but I was surprised that Kaye was dating someone like Scott. She normally liked the tall lean guys.

"And this is *my* date, Darius," Vanessa chimed in. "We work together."

I shook his hand. He was a presentable looking guy. Nothing to pick up the phone and call mama about, but he seemed nice. He was the same height as Vanessa and was a little on the chunky side. He had a boyish face that added some attraction to him.

"Nice to meet you," he said. I nodded and smiled.

"Same here." I frowned as I peered out toward the parking lot. "I thought I saw another person with y'all?"

"Oh yeah," Kaye said with a giggle, and then Vanessa started chuckling too.

"You guys been tossing back a few before you got here?" I asked suspiciously as my eyes squinted. I gestured with my hand as if I were holding a cup and taking a sip.

"Maybe a few," Vanessa said, "but we're fine. We're not gonna embarrass you or nothing like that."

"Good, because the mayor's inside."

"Really??" Darius said. "I have some things I'd like to discuss with him." He adjusted his bright red bowtie and shifted nervously in place.

"No you don't," I politely hinted for him to leave the mayor alone.

Kaye held her head down and chuckled. I just stared vacantly at him and prayed silently that he wouldn't bump into the mayor all evening.

"I'm tired of the potholes. And another thing, why aren't there any street signs in Southeast? No wonder people get lost here all the time." Darius then commented in a hushed tone, "yeah, he needs to know."

I glared at Vanessa and she just shrugged quickly so Darius wouldn't see her.

The tall dark figure finally made his way through the parking lot and in our direction. The silhouette was lean and walked stealthily as if the event wouldn't start until he made it inside the building.

"Who is that?" I whispered as I leaned in to ask Kaye.

Just then, he had gotten closer. I took a huge gulp and widened my eyes. For a moment, I had caught a hot flash and thought I was about to faint. My smooth, problem-free evening was destined to get rocky from here on out. I needed to think of some sort of quick story to get me out of this mess! *Why him? Why right now?* I thought. Kaye kept smiling as if she'd just won a bake-off, but I wanted to take her by the shoulders and shake her wildly, then explain to her that this was neither a good time nor place for a mini-reunion.

"Ahh, Sula," the figure said as he took my hand and kissed it softly. He looked good in his tuxedo and I thought that I would melt like an ice cube on Miami Beach when his soft lips caressed my skin. "Remember me?"

"Pedro, how could I forget?"

"Doesn't he look great?" Kaye was about to bust out of her gown with enthusiasm.

"Dashing," was all I could muster. I immediately thought about Ray and what to say to whom to explain this. What I had to do was avoid one of them for the rest of the night, and since Pedro was late, it would be him. "Well, why don't you guys grab something to eat and I'll see you inside." I turned to walk away, but Pedro gently pulled me back by my arm.

"What's your hurry? I thought you'd be happy to see me again. Especially since I never got that kiss from pool," he began strumming my hand with his fingertips like he were playing a harp. His deep accented voice was sending tiny electric shocks throughout my entire body.

"I am glad to see you, but it's just that I'm *working* this event too, so I can't socialize too much. So go have fun!"

"It's okay. We socialize after," he kissed me on the cheek and held my hand. I chuckled nervously and shot a threatening glance at Kaye that went ignored.

"Kaye? Vanessa? I need to talk to you," I sang out. I walked away from Pedro and flashed another smile before pulling Vanessa and Kaye out onto the terrace.

"Okay, you don't have to thank me," Kaye rambled, "I know. I know. He's fine and you're glad we invited him out, right? Child, Pedro looks good enough to put on a napkin and eat, don't he? You put Pedro's card in my purse instead of Manuel's. How funny is that? Damn! I wish Manuel wasn't gay. Why are all the fine ones, you know...*happy*?"

"Kaye, will you shut up?" I quietly yelled.

Kaye erased the smile from her face and put her hand on her hip. She looked at Vanessa, then back at me. "What's wrong? I thought you'd be glad. As fine as he is."

Vanessa nodded in agreement and said, "That Spanish guy is fine, girl."

I sighed and shook my head. I reached my hands out in an attempt to gently choke them. Kaye slapped my hand away and mumbled a few expletives while Vanessa backed away slightly from my approaching grasp.

"What's wrong?" Vanessa asked.

"You ladies remember Ray?" I began rambling utterances of my own to my two friends. "The one I met at the club? The sports agent? The fine dark brother? The one that I actually went out on a date with? The dude that jokingly proposed to me less than an hour ago? The one that's going out of town tomorrow and wanted to spend some time with me after this event is over? Well, he's *here*!"

They both looked at each other dumbfounded as they digested my mini-rant.

"Oh this is gonna be good as hell!" Kaye finally blared as she hopped around like a teen at a Nicki Minaj concert.

"Kaye, how could you say that?" I whimpered. "I like Ray, but yes I'm attracted to Pedro too. Who wouldn't be? Pedro has that Latin fire. Ooo wee! But I like Ray! What am I gonna do?"

"Just fake a cramp and leave," Kaye suggested, as if that works for her every time.

"I can't do that! This is *my* event!"

Just then I heard a sexy male voice say my name.

"Sula?"

I turned quickly as if I was a child that had just gotten caught writing their name on the wall by a disgruntled parent.

"Yes?"

"Oh, excuse me, I didn't mean to interrupt," Ray apologized.

In my peripheral vision, I could see Kaye nudge Vanessa several times in the arm. I suppose that was my cue to do the introductions.

"Oh, you didn't. Let me introduce you. Ray, these are my girls, Kaye and Vanessa."

"Well, it's nice to meet you ladies. I got cornered by some dude who's a guitarist. I think he was about to ask for a small loan," he told me with a disgusted expression while pointing back inside the hall. "Oh and I think I saw a piece that I want to buy."

"Okay, I'll be in there in just a second, honey," I assured him. "Have another glass of champagne!"

"Okay, I'll see you inside. Ladies . . ." he smiled and then walked away.

"Now I see why you are in such a fuss about this whole thing!" Kaye said. "He is *fine*, girl. I don't know how you manage to pull all these fine men, but *he* was fine. I'm talking chocolate double dipped, Oreo cookie fine."

"Eh," Vanessa shrugged, "he's no Darius." Vanessa shared with a wink of her eye.

"Okay, well, just try to keep Pedro occupied and outta my face for tonight," I instructed them both.

My palms were getting sweaty and my breathing became labored. I tried to refocus on the event at hand and the artists, not this ridiculous situation with two extremely handsome men that did not need to know about each other. I had decided that this would be a great time to sneak away to the restroom. Maybe in this make shift sanctuary I could get my thoughts together. I peered over at the grandfather clock. We had another hour and a half to go. I secretly hoped that I could keep things together until the gala was over. The quintet had taken a 15-minute break, so for a moment all that was heard was constant chatter among the guests.

Just as I made my way down the corridor and out of sight of the crowd, Pedro came running up behind me like he was passing me a baton in a track and field event.

"Where you go?"

"To the restroom. Is that okay with you?"

"I still wan' my kiss."

"Um, Pedro, did you take a look at the artwork at all yet?" I looked around nervously.

"No, I no' into art," he said with a shrug as he closed his eyes and shook his head at the notion which seemed beneath his taste.

"Really? So why did you come?"

"I came to see my Sula. I came for my kiss, maybe more," he leaned in closer and tried to nibble on my exposed shoulder. I backed up but ended right against the cold marble wall that caused my back to arch. I guess Pedro thought that poking my chest out from the sensation of the marble against my back was a cue for him to continue flirting, because he tried to kiss my shoulder again.

"Pedro? No . . ." I put my hands up to allow space between me and him. He was being really frisky. "This is not the place, and it's definitely not the time."

"Que hora es?" he laughed raucously. I looked around embarrassed for him.

"Don't get cute. I have to go to the little girl's room."

He ignored my comment and wrapped an arm around me. He puckered up and pulled me close to him with a strong movement. I backed my face away from his and tucked in my lips. I wasn't about to believe he was this hard up. What was this mofo's problem? I put both hands on his chest and tried to push him back. He still had his lips puckered, and neck outstretched awaiting a kiss.

"Will you back up??" I ordered with one fist balled and arm cocked, ready to strike a hard blow to his sternum.

He backed up and smiled. "Hard to get, I like that."

I held up my fist, shook it in front of his nose and pretended I was smiling through gnashed teeth. "You *won't* like it in a minute. Now, I'm serious. I need to go to the restroom and this behavior is not appropriate here. Excuse me." I turned to walk away, but he thrust his arm against the wall blocking my escape route.

"I just wan' one kiss."

"No."

"Please? One and I leave you."

"You're going to leave me alone with or without the kiss. Now move."

"Uh uh," he teased and chuckled. His behavior was far from charming and way past annoying. Whatever chance he had with me, was now completely gone. I didn't take too kindly to men who didn't understand what 'no' meant. By this time, I could feel my blood racing faster through my veins as my body pumped adrenalin rapidly to my brain. I seriously considered punching him in the rib cage just so I could get a moment to myself as I had originally planned. I wasn't a violent person, but Pedro was certainly flirting with a beat down. I turned to go in the opposite direction, but he blocked it with his other arm and had me trapped.

"You've never been bitten before have you?" I said with a serious expression. I could've bitten through that rented tux and right into his flesh.

"Yes! I like!!"

"Pedro? Really? Do you mind? I'd like to leave now."

"One kiss, then you go."

I sighed heavily and took a few seconds to think about it. If it meant getting him out of my face without me having to put my shoe print in his ass, one peck wouldn't hurt.

"Just one! Then you gots to go!" I reaffirmed holding up a single finger in front of his face.

"Yes."

His face softened with seduction. He leaned toward me, and planted a long closed mouth kiss on my lips. Afterward, he backed away slothfully, dropping his arms to his side as he looked deep into my eyes. All of the childishness had left him as he gazed at me. My eyes locked with his for a brief moment, and then I cleared my throat which reminded me that I needed to go to the restroom. I softly wiped my lips and turned in the direction that headed back to the party. I wasn't really sure why I had turned that way, since the bathroom was in the other direction. I supposed that wonderful kiss had kind of scrambled my mind a tad bit. I smoothed out my hair and looked up . . .

"What's going on here, Sula?"

My stomach dropped to my ankles and then felt as though it was trying to climb its way back to its rightful place, because there he stood before me . . . Ray.

"Ray? Hi! This is not what it looks like. At all."

Pedro moved closer to stand beside me and placed his hand on my shoulder. I glared at him as he looked down at me smiling. His gesture hadn't made the situation look any differently than what I was about to convince Ray of. I took Pedro's hand off of me and walked toward Ray. His smiling, jovial expression that he'd had earlier that evening had turned harder than any face on Mt. Rushmore.

"Ray, it was nothing. He stopped me when I was on my way to the bathroom. He wouldn't let me go unless I gave him a kiss." I turned to Pedro. "Will you tell him?"

"Tell him what?"

Ray still said nothing. He just looked at me as if he'd caught me in a lie. The only thing that was wrong with this picture was that I wasn't lying. Had Ray rounded the corner 30 seconds earlier, that kiss would never have taken place and he would've seen me trying to escape.

"Ray, please? I'm not making this up. I hardly know him."

"Yeah that makes sense," he sarcastically said.

"That's not what I meant. He was blocking my way and told me that he would let me go if I gave him a kiss. Had you shown up earlier, you would've seen that."

"It looked like you were enjoying his ultimatum."

"I don't care about him!"

Then Pedro chimed in with his wisecrack, "That's no' what you said last night."

I couldn't believe that Pedro was lying and trying to bust me. I shut my eyes securely and shook my head frantically in complete disbelief. My mouth couldn't form the words fast enough.

"WHAT?" I yelled. I supposed my voice was a little too thunderous because the chatter amongst the guest had ceased slightly before starting up again. I walked over to Pedro halting my face just inches from his. "There will NEVER be a last night between us, no matter how much you pray for it. You need to leave Pedro. I mean it! Get the hell outta here! You got three seconds before I get security to haul your ass out the back with the rest of the trash!! GO!!"

With both hands on my hips, I stood my ground waiting for him to leave. His comedic expression faded drastically. For a second there, I'd thought he shrunk about two feet as he quietly brushed past me and then Ray. I turned to make sure that he was leaving and saw a few guests gathered at the end of the hallway. Ray stood there staring at me pokerfaced but at this point, I'm sure I was angrier than he.

"Sula . . ." he started.

"I still have to go pee!" I turned around and stomped down the hall to the restroom, my heels digging into the marble tile loudly along the way. I busted through the door and slammed it shut.

"Ooooo!" I groaned aloud once I got inside safely.

There I was babbling to Ray as if he were some seasoned detective. I had done nothing wrong! Matter of fact, I couldn't believe that Ray was standing there waiting for an explanation. We went out once and there are no rings on *these* fingers! And that conniving Pedro with his, '*that's not what you said last night*' comment. Why would he say something like that? As if making that statement would've gotten rid of his competition, thus clearing the way for him to get closer to me. Then to top it all off, I made a complete idiot of myself! I was not about to go back out there and carry on as if everything was normal. But I knew I couldn't stay in this bathroom for the rest of the night, no matter how much I wanted to.

I took several deep breaths in and out to relax myself. I know that while I was in that hallway, my pressure had probably gone up to 10,000 over 80. I turned the cold water on the faucet and snatched a stack of paper towels from the dispenser. I ran them under the water and patted my face. The scene replayed over and over in my mind. Thank goodness Vanessa and Kaye weren't there to witness the scene; they would never let me live that incident down. Just as my relief began to sustain my anger, there was a knock on the door.

"Sula? Sula are you okay?"

It was Kaye. Well so much for not having the incident thrown back up in my face.

"I'm fine."

"Let us in."

"Hurry up, girl before more people start coming down this hallway," Vanessa whispered through the door.

Before opening the door, I patted my hair and smoothed out my dress, trying to give the impression that I was perfectly fine. They rushed in and quickly closed the door behind them. Vanessa reopened it a bit and peeked through the crevice to see if anyone was behind them. She breathed a sigh of relief, closed the door and locked it. She leaned her head backward and put her hand over her heart and let out another heavy sigh.

"What are you two doing?" I asked.

"Girl, what happened?" Kaye wondered. She swept my hair back into place with her fingertips. Vanessa just stood there, staring at me as if I had just landed from a distant planet.

"Yeah, Pedro rushed out of here and didn't say a word to anybody," Vanessa volunteered.

"I just have one question," I started. I put my hand over my forehead and tried to ignore the headache that I could feel coming on.

"Yes, we could hear your loud mouth all the way up front," Kaye said as she turned to wash her hands.

"I knew it," I said with disappointment, "may as well pack up and go back to Africa . . . for good this time."

Vanessa blurted out, "Please. It wasn't that bad. Most of the people weren't even paying attention."

"Except for when you told him that 'there will never be a last night between us, no matter how much he prayed for it'," Kaye retorted. "Oh and when you called him trash, basically."

*   *   *   *

We stepped out of the bathroom. Much to my surprise, Ray was still in the hallway waiting—along with a small group of women in line to use the facilities. As soon as we came out of the restroom, all of the women stared at us as though we had all been selected as Miss Universe and they were the first runner-ups. I was hoping that Kaye wouldn't address the rude stares we received and just ignore them. Much to my surprise, she did.

Ray still looked a touch upset and probably wanted a bit more of an explanation. But unfortunately, the explanation that I gave him was all there was to it. I thought it was really sweet that he waited for me in the hallway until I came out of the bathroom.

"You're still here?" Kaye asked. A hint of embarrassment veiled Ray's face for a moment as the women that were waiting in line glanced in his direction. I guess they wondered exactly how long he'd been waiting. "He's a keeper, Sula."

"We'll meet you out front," Vanessa said in a whisper as she locked her arm into Kaye's and pulled her away.

I stood before Ray waiting to hear his thoughts orally.

"Can we go somewhere and talk?" he breathed the words out.

"Sure, I apologize for keeping you waiting," I told him, trying to feel out the measure of his disappointment with the whole situation.

We went towards the front of the building and into the parking lot. There were a few people leaving.

He nodded as if he understood completely. I took a deep breath and braced myself for the worst. Worst-case scenario: tonight would be the last night we'd see each other, based on the kiss Pedro blackmailed me for. On the flipside of that coin, he'd understand that tonight was just a terrible misunderstanding and we could put this tragic event behind us and move forward. I was without a shadow of a doubt praying for the latter.

"Sula, I think I owe you an apology."

"Oh?" I was surprised. I didn't expect him to say that. Prayer works.

"Yes. I know that you're not my woman, as much as I'd like for you to be, and I had no right coming off the way I did to you. Now, I'll admit, I was upset. The story did seem a bit far-fetched, but I believe you," he took my hand into his, "you accept my apology?"

"Yes, I do. Thank you, Ray." I smiled as my other hand covered his. "It wasn't my intent to hurt you in any way. Pedro was someone that I met about a week or so ago, I hadn't spoken to him since then, my girls just brought him up here without me knowing. They were trying to surprise me."

"Yeah, Vanessa told me about it. Besides you look like you were about to stomp old boy in the ground," he gave a light chuckle, "with your fine self." He showed off his bright smile that was surrounded by his soft lips. My heart overflowed with warmth at the sight of his smile again.

"I thought I was going to too. I'm really sorry about this. It was all a terrible misunderstanding."

Our soft chortles had faded smoothly as we both silently reflected on tonight's events.

"Well," he began, "I'm gonna go on home and get myself packed. I've got an early flight tomorrow. I'll call you while I'm there or when I get back."

"Well, I'm praying you will do both."

"Yes. Both." He pulled me toward him. I lifted my face so my lips would meet his. This kiss would serve as reassurance that he was okay with everything that had happened. I couldn't begin to imagine what I would've done if the tables were turned or even if I would've been as understanding as he. I guessed I owed some thanks to Vanessa and Kaye. I didn't want to picture how the scene would've played out if those two weren't around to have my back.

I took a deep breath and prepared myself for a nice, long, warm kiss from Ray. He pulled me toward him, placed his hand carefully behind my head and caressed my neck gently with his thumb. I looked deep into his eyes. Then, he kissed me – right on my forehead.

"Thanks for inviting me out. I'll call you when I get there tomorrow." He flashed a wave, smiled and walked away. My legs felt like two Roman pillars pounded into the cement as I stood there and watched him make his way to his car.

Chapter Six - The Fifth Wheel

The gala wasn't a total bust, despite what went down with Pedro in the hallway. By Wednesday we had received 200 separate orders with varying quantities. By my calculations, the event was a *total* success. The day after the event, I got a call from Ray. He made it to Sacramento just fine. He called me once he got settled in and said that he would be meeting with the athlete's coach later that evening and that he would be thinking of me.

Ditto for me.

My mind replayed thoughts of the grandfather kiss Ray gave me to the forehead. I mean even though I'm grumbling, it was still a sweet gesture, so I'll just leave it at that. Besides, I had other things to focus on besides that innocent kiss goodnight and the whole event in general.

I picked up a stack of receipts and was about to tally them up when I noticed the red flashing light from my answering machine indicating that I had messages. I had on some shorts and a tank top and gathered a bunch of books from my home office into a pile. Just as I had reached over to grab the phone, it rang. The loud ringer frightened me so bad, I instinctively placed my hand over my heart to keep it from jumping out of my chest. I answered the phone.

"Hello?"

"Hey, it's Ray. Are you missing me?"

"Of course," I replied. "I know you're missing me, so I won't even ask."

He chuckled lightly, "you're right about that one. I'll actually be back a day early and I want to see you. Can you scoop me up from the airport?"

"Sure! I'll pick you up on Sunday then," I offered.

"Sula Mae," he started, "that sounds like a plan."

"Wait a minute. Did you just call me *Sula Mae*?"

"Yeah!" He laughed. "Don't you like that name?"

"Negative. Especially since it's not mine!" I teased. "Where'd you get that from?"

"It fits. That's gonna be my nickname for you from now on. Sula Mae. I'll talk to you soon, sweetheart. Miss me."

I put the phone back in the cradle and stepped into the kitchen to make a snack. Just as I had my face buried in the refrigerator trying to find something quick to.eat, the phone rang again. I closed the fridge, picked up the phone and answered with an annoyed sigh.

"Hello?"

"Hey girl, it's 'Nessa."

"What up, chick?"

"I got something to tell ya."

"You're pregnant?"

She laughed so loud in my ear that I pulled the receiver away a good six or seven inches.

"Naa, silly. I met someone."

"That's nice Vanessa," I said flatly.

"Well dang, you ain't gotta be so happy for your girl."

"Vanessa, every time you tell me you've met someone, you're dumping him after a week or so."

"That's not true," she defended. "I do not!"

"Okay, what about little Malcolm X-cess weight that you brought to the art exhibit? Wearing his little red bow tie. What was his name? Devious?" I laughed and strolled back into the kitchen. I opened the door to the fridge and peered inside.

"*Darius.* And he was just someone that I work with. Nothing there."

"Yeah, right. Okay, so what's this new guy like?"

"He's cute!" She giggled. "Oops, hold on, my phone is beeping."

She placed me on hold. Vanessa had an uncanny knack for calling me when I was always in the middle of something.

"Girl," she started, "that's him. I'll holla at you later on."

I hung up the phone and went back into the kitchen where I perused the cabinets for "quick fixes" like crackers, or granola bars, but I didn't see a thing. I needed to do some grocery shopping badly. All I had were spices and what I like to call "back up" food, which was food that I would only eat if there was a nuclear holocaust – like bran cereal.

I needed to go to the grocery store, but I couldn't go on an empty stomach. I'd end up buying more than what I had a desire to eat and the grocery bill would be like $400. I picked up the phone to see if I could catch Kaye. She's probably out with some dude, I thought. Just as I decided to call her, my cell phone rang from inside of my purse.

"This is Sula." I answered in my professional voice. The cell was for business purposes as well, and if someone wanted to buy art at two in the morning, I'd be available to take their order.

"Girl, it's past quitting time! What are you doing answering your phone like that for?"

"Kaye? My God, I was *just* about to call you. I've got to get something to eat and haven't got a thing in this house!" I confessed, looking around my townhouse as if it were the center of a forest and I had just eaten my last can of beans.

"Son of a gun. We must have ESPN or something. I'm around the corner and I have some Chinese food. Feel like grubbing? I never got a chance to say thanks for inviting me out to the art thing-a-ma-jig."

"No problem, homie. Well, you know Vanessa met a man," I mentioned in a flat tone.

"Yeah, she told me. Oh! We should all go out. That way we can meet him. I'll bring Justin!"

"Great." I gulped hard because Ray was out of town and I always hated being a third wheel. Or in this case a fifth wheel. Since this new guy seemed to mean a lot to Vanessa, I would have to swallow my insecurity and support her new relationship. I had a feeling it was going to be an interesting affair.

*   *   *   *

As I started for the entrance to The Cheesecake Factory, I saw that Kaye and her date were waiting for everyone in the foyer. Kaye was staring at the entrance and stood a few feet away from the guy she was with.

"Hey girl! You look good!" Kaye said and greeted me with a hug. During the hug, she whispered, "Thank God you're here."

"Okay... Oh! You look great too!" She had on a jean outfit that I would soon be borrowing.

"I know!" she blurted out with a chuckle. "Oh, Sula this is Justin."

"Nice to meet you," Justin said as he extended his hand.

"Same here. Soooo, Vanessa's late?" I asked while looking around at the customers in the foyer.

"Naturally. But it's cool, I already put us on the list. They should be calling us in a few minutes." Kaye responded while looking at the mall entrance.

"So Sula, Kaye tells me you own your own art gallery," Justin started. I kind of had an idea of where this was going. By the look of his shoes, he seemed to have expensive taste and probably knew his art. He more than likely had a nice collection of his own.

"Yes, I do. Do you collect art?"

"No, I'm not a collector. But I am looking to purchase a few pieces for my new house. I just moved in a month ago and the bare walls are screaming for some art." He pulled Kaye close to him by her waist. She smiled slightly and patted his hand as she gently moved it away, then she turned her attention back to the mall entrance.

"Well, you should check out my website and see which pieces you'd like. I offer all of my friends of friends the same zero percent discount!" I chuckled and he smiled with a nod as I handed him a business card. I always use that line to let people know not to be expecting the art for free. I mean, after all, I *was* a businesswoman that wanted to *stay* in business. Kaye looked at me with a disgusted smirk as she threw her eyes up to the ceiling. I guess she was tired of my "zero percent discount" line after all this time.

"Kaye?" The hostess intervened, "your table is ready."

We headed into the restaurant and took our seats. As soon as we got to our booth, Kaye flopped in her seat and rested her chin on the heel of her hand. Something was definitely up and I needed to know what was wrong.

"Justin, can you excuse us while we go to the restroom?" I asked him. During the misdst of my question, Kaye had stood to her feet. Apparently she was relieved that I picked up on her cue and realized that we needed a minute alone to talk.

"Oh sure," Justin said. He looked up at Kaye and placed a gentle hand on her back. She moved over to the side away from his touch and started toward the restroom, leaving me behind.

As soon as we made our way to the restroom, Kaye sighed hard and said, "We are going to have to cut this date as short as possible." She started pacing and shaking her head.

"What? Why?"

"Okay, I've known Justin for a little bit, right? So, I mean, he *is* a little cutie. I figured we could get busy before coming here . . ."

I tilted my head in disapproval.

"Save it, Sula. Anyway, his cute ass ain't got nothing to work with! Then on top of that, he's a preemie!" She began scrubbing her hands feverishly creating a soapy mess as if to rid his scent and touch from her skin.

"Damn. A two hump chump," I confirmed.

"And then had the nerve to think he *really* did something. Why are preemies like that? That made it worse! Now he's feeling all close, affectionate and attached. He won't stop with the - ugh! I don't even want him touching me. What a mistake! What a terrible terrible mistake!"

I was silent as I watched her scrub her hands. She turned the faucet off and I handed her a fistful of paper towels.

"Well?" she started, "say something!!"

"Like what?" I asked as I checked my lipstick in the mirror. "I didn't tell you to sleep with homeboy. You need to start taking some more cold showers in the evenings with your little fast tail."

She laughed a little, "You know what, Sula? Just pray that I don't bust his ass out tonight if he says or does something that rubs me the wrong way. You know me, I can't hold anything in."

"Yeah," I sighed, "I know you."

When we returned to the table, Vanessa and her date were there and she looked like the belle of the ball with two men flanking her sides. Her man had his eyes glued to Kaye's and my breasts when we approached the table.

"Kaye, Sula?" Vanessa was fidgeting in her seat with excitement like she couldn't wait to use the bathroom, "*This* is Kenard."

Kenard looked Kaye and me up and down.

"Damn, Vanessa," he said in a deafening tone, "I didn't know you had some fine assed girlfriends. How y'all doing? Mmphf. Damn." He licked his chops.

Instantly offended, Kaye looked at Kenard and gritted her teeth. She took her seat next to Justin and flatly responded, "Fine."

"I'm good." I sat down and glared at him suspiciously as I settled into my seat.

"So which one is Kaye and which one is Sula? Naa let me guess. The lovely lady in the jean outfit is Sula. You look like you'd have an exotic name like that. You fine as shit baby girl." He pointed to me, "and you're Kaye, right? Damn look at those eyes."

"Wrong!" Kaye blurted. I could tell that Kaye was about to take her sexual frustrations with Justin out on poor Kenard.

"Oh, my bad. Didn't mean to offend you, sexy."

"Ain't he cute, y'all?" Vanessa interjected as she hugged herself closer to Kenard. He smiled, showing off a gold cap on one of his teeth. Kaye narrowed her eyes at him.

I pretended to read the contents of the menu, but was privately conversing with the restaurant gods that we wouldn't get thrown out and for the wait staff not to sabotage the food.

"So uh, what do you do?" I asked Kenard.

"I work for the phone company, Cat Eyes. I do repair," he summed up. "Where's that waitress? I'm hungrier than four inmates up in this piece."

"He's so cute! Have you guys been here long?" Vanessa asked me.

Kaye mumbled, "Cat Eyes?"

"About ten minutes. It wasn't long," I answered Vanessa.

"Man, I refuse to be on time!" Kenard offered. "The party don't start until I get there anyway!"

Vanessa chuckled uncontrollably, "He's so cute!"

Kaye was staring at Vanessa the entire time with an inspecting demeanor. Justin was too busy taking in Kaye's features to even care about what was going on. He was even playing with her hair. While Vanessa thought Kenard was a hoot, he was slowly rubbing me the wrong way. I tried desperately to give him the benefit of the doubt, but he was truly pushing it. By this time, the bubbly blonde waitress came over to our table.

"Hi, my name is Candi, I'll be your waitress this evening and I'd like to tell . . ."

"Candi, huh?" Kenard rudely interrupted, "when the last time you been sucked on, Candi? You can rot my teeth, girl."

She turned beet red.

"Will you shut up for a second, so she can tell us what the specials are?" Kaye scorned.

"Oh, my bad, sexy," he held both of his hands up in surrender as he apologized to Kaye.

Candi gave an embarrassing chuckle and quickly fired off the list of specials. She took our drink orders without any further interruptions and hurried away from the table.

In an effort to ease the tension, I decided to spark some light conversation. Actually, I just wanted to be nosey and find out how and where Vanessa and Kenard met. They seemed like the Odd Couple. From what I gathered so far, Vanessa thought he was cute and funny. Oh, and yes, she thought he was "cute". I guess she couldn't find another word. Every chance she got, that was her one word description of Kenard. I wanted to beat her over the head with a thesaurus. Strangely, Kenard didn't comment too much on Vanessa.

"So how'd you guys meet?" Justin asked them.

"Well . . . it was kind of funny how we met . . . um, we sorta . . ." Vanessa started.

"We met off of the internet," he volunteered. "I saw her picture and was like damn, I got to holla at that! When she sent me a full body shot, oh shit! I already had my game plan mapped out. Right leg up, left leg down, BANG!" he thrust his mid section in one hard single motion and put his arm around her. He smiled at us and kissed Vanessa sloppily on the cheek.

Vanessa bashfully giggled and playfully shoved him. With that gesture, maybe he had her left leg up instead. It was clear that event had already occurred.

"See, I couldn't do that, "Justin stated. "There are some crazy people out here."

"Case and point sitting right at this damn table," Kaye said as she pointed in Kenard's direction without him even noticing. Kaye was quite skilled at doing that. I begged her to teach me that tactic. Kaye could talk about someone, even insult them, with them being just inches away and they would be unable to hear her. However, everyone else would be able to hear every word clearly. That's a gift.

"All you gotta do Dog is pray about it," Kenard hypocritically concluded.

We continued to listen to Kenard's antics until the waitress returned and took our orders. Sure enough once Candi returned, Kenard performed again.

"Y'all got franks and beans?" Kenard looked at the waitress seriously once the loudness of his voice settled on our ears like dust.

There was a couple in the booth next to us and the girl turned her head slightly in our direction, then leaned toward her date. I suspected that she told him that Kenard had just asked for beans and franks. The brother peered over at us and let out a single laugh. His date shook her head.

"Um, no. We do have andouille sausage that we use for our jambalaya dish and could probably give you a side of black beans," she nodded as if he were a seven-year old.

"Naa, that's all right. I'll take the chicken drummettes," he said. He then folded his menu and shoved it toward Candi.

"It would've been nice if the ladies could've ordered first . . ." Kaye said to Kenard.

"Baby, I'm sure he didn't mean it," Justin said in Kenard's defense and gave Kaye a peck on the cheek. Kaye shot Justin a damning look and gnashed her teeth as she spoke.

"Don't defy me, Justin," Kaye said with a slight jerk of her head. She then smiled and told the waitress, "I'll have the Shrimp Alfredo."

"I'll take the crab cakes, with a side of steamed broccoli. I'm in the mood for seafood too," Vanessa said.

"You need to leave that seafood alone," Kenard started, "your belly is starting to jiggle more. Hell, you just need to stop eating for a few weeks, babe."

Vanessa smiled and shoved Kenard playfully, "Kenard!"

That was my cue to interpose. I could no longer tolerate his disrespectfulness toward my girl while Vanessa was just sitting there laughing it off unapprised.

"Excuse me, Candi," I spoke up, "could you give us just a few more minutes please?"

"Sure!" she scurried off.

"Um, Kenard, I think I must say this and pardon me for doing this in front of everyone at the table, but I think you are being a bit disrespectful to my girl."

"Yup," Kaye agreed and sipped her water.

"Sula!" Vanessa interrupted.

"No, Vanessa, you need to hush," Kaye stopped her from speaking any further by holding up a quieting palm. "Go 'head, Sula."

Vanessa closed her mouth that was gaped open and slouched back in her seat. Justin removed his arm from around Kaye's shoulder. This was the first time he wasn't touching or trying to touch her.

"Kenard, your flirting was bad enough, but to talk about her body negatively in front of everyone here is just plain rude."

"Who you think you is?" he retaliated.

"*Excuse* me?"

"No, hold up. I got this Kenard. Sula," Vanessa started in a defensive tone, "*I'm* the one that likes Kenard. *I'm* the one who thinks he's cute. You don't have to like him. He's not perfect, but we have a nice time together. So

I would appreciate it if you kept your comments about him to yourself. Now, can we continue our evening?"

"That's right! You tell her baby!" Kenard said, sealing Vanessa's statement with a kiss on her cheek and a slight embrace. "Her *and* Miss Bougie could learn a thing or two from you, boo."

"What did you just say, ignorant?" Kaye moved in closer to hear him a little better.

"Whoa, Kaye. That is uncalled for and is not very lady-like," Justin said as he shook his head and looked at me to co-sign his statement. Unfortunately, Justin was out on that limb alone.

"You need to stay out of it, Limp Dick McSpeedy!"

Justin looked down in his lap ashamed, as Kenard laughed. I almost choked. Vanessa shook her head in disbelief as she bit down on her lip to contain herself from vocalizing her thoughts.

"Okay, okay," I intervened. "You know what Kaye, if Vanessa is happy with . . . with *Kenard*, then I guess we should be happy for her. That's her business."

I was trying to calm things down before Kaye blew a gasket. I wanted to leave to be honest and coincidentally Kaye shared my sentiments, because she hooked her purse onto her shoulder preparing to leave.

"Well, Sula, I'm glad *you* feel that way," Kaye stood up. "I'm leaving. I'll damnit walk home if I have to."

"It's 25 miles! Kaye, baby, just wait . . ." Justin held on to her arm.

Kenard sat back grinning the entire time. My stomach was flip-flopping and my palms had gotten clammy. I wasn't going to let Kaye walk and certainly was about to roll with her. But why did I feel obligated to Vanessa? After all, it was our idea to do a mass date. I looked at the exit and at the customers who were investigating the drama at our table. I swayed nervously in my seat.

"Kaye, have a seat. It was our idea, so let's not be rude," I pleaded with her. She stood for a moment longer in contemplation before she scorned.

"Are you crazy, Sula?" she stared at me.

"I guess," I responded and then thought about it. "No, you're right. Let's go." I grabbed my purse and stood up. Vanessa looked dumbfounded while Kenard reached for the bread.

"Guys, wait!" Vanessa pleaded.

"Naa, we're leaving," Kaye said and she slightly shoved me toward the exit. Justin jumped up to remain with Kaye. I saw Vanessa nudge Kenard and then swept her hand in a gesture signaling him to leave with her.

*   *   *   *

We all gathered in the foyer of the mall entrance. I wasn't about to watch Kaye be carted off in a cab, so I insisted that she ride with me. Justin pathetically tried to convince her to ride back with him so he could make it up to her. It was sickening how Kaye could be so ruthless to these men and have them eating from the palm of her hands after she'd chewed them up and spit them out. Needless to say, Kaye had successfully ignored him. To add insult to injury, she had verbally kicked him while she had his ego kissing the canvas.

"Look Justin, I'm just not interested! You just can't please me sexually. It was wrong on so many levels, okay?"

She walked toward the parking lot even though she didn't know where my car was. I gave a sympathetic look to Justin, who was clearly crushed by her comment and probably by how loud she delivered it. He turned and walked away. I looked at Vanessa and Kenard to say goodbye. Kenard was busy watching a group of half-dressed 20-something year olds who were clearly inebriated and giggly. Vanessa sort of sneered at me and I just flashed a wave and told her "later." It was clearly time for me to retire from the title of "peacemaker".

Chapter Seven - What's Your Problem?

I decided to have a small surprise for Ray when I picked him up from the airport that afternoon. I had an assortment of fresh fruit for him. I hoped that he liked my surprise. I was looking like I stepped straight out of the seventies, with my faded patched boot cut jeans and low cropped peace tie-dyed shirt. I was starting to redevelop my abs and felt like showing them off a bit today. I pulled my hair in a high bun.

He looked absolutely exhausted when I spotted him rounding the corner from the terminal. He let out a yawn and then his eyes met mine. I would've paid money for that smile that I received. He had a faded brown leather shoulder bag lopping at his side.

"Sula Mae!" he yelled out.

A few people looked in our direction. I smiled at him and held up a single fist while I shook it at him.

He found some energy and sped up toward me. He dropped his bag to the floor and grabbed me with one arm, picked me up and spun me around. I yelped until he put me down.

"Hey, baby!" I said. "Damn you look sexy as hell."

This was definitely a passionate kiss moment. He leaned in and kissed me – on the forehead. Again! My smile faded slightly as I looked down at the container of fruit in my hands.

"Thanks for picking me up, baby. That hairstyle looks so good on you." He picked up his bag and threw his arm around me and carted me off with him to the baggage claim.

"I brought you some fruit. I thought you'd like it." I looked into his eyes to try to read his thoughts. They emulated that he was happy and that was that. He pulled me closer to him and kissed me on the cheek.

"You are such a sight for sore eyes," he told me. "How have you been?"

"I've been good. How was your scouting?"

"Long, but I think I'll have some good athletes under my belt. I could use the clients, you know?" He gripped the side of my waist and jiggled it. That's one of my ticklish spots, but I didn't feel like laughing right then. "So what'd you do while I was gone, Sula?"

We had reached the baggage claim and he was eyeing the conveyor belt for his bags.

"Hung out with friends and caught up on work. Nothing special."

His bag came around and he snatched it up. "Alright, let's go."

* * * *

"Do you want me to drop you at home so you can get settled?" I asked as we loaded ourselves in the car. We had planned on going out later this evening. But now all of a sudden, I preferred to just take him home and run some errands.

"Yeah, I want to get a nap in before we roll out this evening. Is seven thirty okay?" He placed his hand on my thigh and I nodded.

"Are you going to be up for that?" I tried to prompt him to back out of our previously made plans for the evening.

"I'm good, sweetheart. I'll pick you up as planned. Cool?"

"Cool," I responded. "I really missed you!" I leaned over and puckered my lips for him to kiss. Okay, I'd be curious to see how he would back out of this overt gesture. He'd have to answer it with at least a "slight" peck on the lips. I closed my eyes and waited to feel his soft lips at least graze mine. Just then a car behind us honked their horn as an indication for me to move out.

"Light's green, Sula," Ray noted.

"Right," I responded and pressed my foot all the way down on the pedal. By this time I was driving like a maniac to haul him off to his house. I didn't understand. I was going to get to the bottom of this and was determined to have some answers by the end of the day. Was he ever going to kiss me again? What was the deal here?

While I was in Ray's neighborhood, I decided to stop by a nearby grocery store to finally get some food for the house since my cupboards had been barren for far too long. As I was in line to check out, I looked over to the next lane at a woman who was in the process of emptying her cart and putting her items on the conveyor belt. She looked a little familiar to me, but I couldn't place her face. I didn't want to stare, but I knew I had seen her some place before.

The teenager behind the register had begun ringing up my groceries. Just as the cashier told me the total cost, the lady in the next lane looked in my direction and slowly passed by me. She stopped and headed toward me.

"Sula? Sula Tyler?" she asked.

"Yeah, that's me." I handed some bills to the cashier. I still couldn't place her face.

"It's me. Pam. Pam Lewis. We worked at the publishing company in Oregon. Remember me?" She smiled wide.

"Yes! Pam! It's nice to see you again!"

She made her way over to me and gave me a hug. The teen was holding out his hand waiting for me to take my change.

"What are you doing all the way over here?" I continued. I accepted my change and was relieved that I wasn't losing my mind. We only had lunch a few times at the publishing company, but I remembered that she was a nice person.

"I got tired of all the rain!" she laughed and pushed her basket filled with bagged groceries toward the exit. "Tired of not finding Mr. Right and just tired of everything! So how have you been? How long have you been here in D.C.?"

"Going on four years," I sighed to show my empathy about the finding Mr. Right part.

"I just got here about four months ago. It is such a relief to see someone that I know!"

By this time, we had made our way to the parking lot.

"Well, let me give you my number. I can show you the town and where all of the hang outs are."

"Uhh, I think I know where most of them are!" she chuckled, "But let's hang out. It's so hard to make friends here. It seems really cliquish." She frowned.

I pulled out a business card from my purse and scribbled my cell number on the back. "I've got a few of my close friends here. Maybe we can all hang out."

"That's sounds like a plan. I'll be calling you soon, I've got to run." She opened her car door and began putting her groceries inside. "It is so nice seeing you."

"Same here! Call me soon."

*   *   *   *

Ray and I went to Utopia's in D.C.. I unfolded my napkin and placed it in my lap. I was starving. The last time I ate that day was before I picked him up from the airport. My mouth was watering for their world famous crab cake. The waiter delivered his Jack & Coke, and my Apple Martini.

"You look great," he told me, "So what'd you do when you dropped me off?"

"Thanks! I just ran some errands. Oh! I bumped into someone that I used to work with at the publishing company back in Portland, Oregon . . ."

He interrupted me, "A guy?"

I stopped and became slightly offended.

"Uh, *no*. A young lady." I hope he wasn't the type of guy that thought he owned me after two dates.

"Oh." He began to butter his bread that the waiter had brought over to us and then sipped his drink.

"Anyway, she just moved here about four months ago."

"Cool. So what's up with your friend?"

"Oh, I don't know, we didn't really get a chance to talk that much today. She and I plan to hang out though."

"No, not *her*," he said pretentiously, "the Spanish guy . . ."

"What do you mean?'" I felt like an impromptu inquisition was about to ensue. For what, I had no idea because Pedro and the kissing incident was a dead issue for me. However, I decided to play his little game, as long as he didn't have any problems playing mine.

"Have you seen him since the art exhibit?"

"Why do you ask?" I said with a smile as I carefully folded my arms.

"Just wondering."

"No. I haven't seen him. But he did call to apologize though. I didn't bother to respond." I informed him. Ray's face was frozen. I guess he wasn't expecting me to be the forthcoming with information regarding Pedro.

"Really?"

"Yes."

He grew silent and stirred his drink around by swirling the glass. He became lost in the whirlpool of liquor.

"Is everything okay?" I asked.

"What?"

"I said is everything okay?"

"Sula," he started, and then took a deep sigh, "I like you, but I didn't like the fact that that Spanish guy was there. I'll admit . . . I was offended." He shifted again and cleared his throat. He turned his glass up and chugged the liquor down in one swig. He then motioned for the waiter to bring another drink to him.

"I understand and I thought we squashed that. So, is that why you haven't kissed me on the mouth since then?"

"What?" His voice raised about two octaves and he looked like someone told him there was cyanide in the drink he just scarfed down. "What are you talking about?"

"Ray, after you saw me and him kiss, which was a misunderstanding, you haven't kissed me since. Well, you did . . . on the forehead." I took a sip of water to calm myself. I had hoped that he would just come clean about his awkward behavior and not give me some lame excuse.

"Sula. You are so smart, you know that?" he chuckled. The waiter set down his drink and asked if we were ready to order. Ray asked him to give us a few more minutes, and then we'd be ready. "Yes, Sula. I didn't want my lips touching yours since his had. I guess it's a male thing."

"No, it's an immature thing."

He looked stunned at my statement, but at least I was being truthful.

"Ray, I explained the situation to you. I didn't even invite him, my friends did. I'm not interested in Pedro."

He looked down, then picked up his glass jiggled it, causing the ice around to make a mild clanking sound.

"I'll admit it, Sula. When I meet someone I like, I have the tendency to lose my head. I want to be the only one. Or at least think that I am."

"Okay, but Ray, you have to realize that I had a life before you. I'm sure you're not strictly flying solo. I mean, you're attractive and intelligent. I'd be an idiot to think that you didn't have any other women in your life or don't have any that are trying to be with you. But I can't focus on that. If it's meant to be between us, it will be. All I can do is be me. Pedro is a dead subject for us. There was and is nothing there. I hope that's something that you can put behind us. I will let you know this though. I do like you. I mean, I really really do."

I placed my hand on his and gave it a gentle squeeze. He looked up at me from the sign of affection as a smile slowly crept on his face.

*   *   *   *

After dinner, Ray and I returned to my house. This was the first time in a month that we had to spend some *real* time together.

"This is a nice place you've got here," he said when he entered. He looked around at all the artwork, sculptures, and little trinkets as if it were his first trip to Disneyland. "Wow, this is some great stuff you've got here."

"Thank you. You can have a seat."

Instead of sitting, he kept walking around the living room taking in my eclectic collection of articles.

"Would you like something to drink?"

"No, I'm alright right now." His eyes were fixed on one of my paintings. I watched him as he studied every line. After a few moments he finally tore himself away from the piece and approached me. "I like your spot. It's very warm and inviting. *That* picture is cool. Who's the artist?"

"Me. I did that when I got back from Africa."

"Ahh man, that's outta sight, baby. I plan to go back there one of these days."

I chuckled, "Thanks. So, tell me more about yourself, Ray."

He smiled, took a deep breath, and began running down his history to me. "Well, you know a lot already. I'm from Delaware. I have two sisters and two brothers.

I'm the next to the youngest. The only one in the family who isn't married. Went to UMass, got my master's in Sports Management from the University of Maryland. I recruit for all sports, baby. Hockey, baseball, football, basketball, and soccer . . . you name it. There have been a few women, but most of them didn't work out because I spend so much time on the road." He looked a little saddened by his comment.

"No one?" I asked.

"There was one girl. She was really special to me. I met her at U of M."

"What happened?"

"The night I was going to propose to her, she told me she had still been seeing her ex and he proposed the day before. Showed me the ring and everything."

"What?!" I couldn't believe my ears.

"Yeah, it was some pretty devastating shit. But that was a long time ago," he leaned forward and ran his fingers through my hair. "I like talking to you. Even on the phone." He scooted over a little closer to me. "I really like you too, Sula."

Just then, he held my face with both of his hands and planted the juiciest and warmest kiss on my lips. It was just what I had been wanting from him for quite some time.

Chapter Eight - Ladies, Meet Chocolate Mocha Munch

"Sula, what are you up to this evening? Let's go check out some strippers!" Pam's voice beamed from the other end of the telephone receiver.

"Strippers? Girl, you are crazy! Well, let me call Kaye and see if she is up for seeing some sweaty men," I suggested.

"Sure the more the merrier. I'll call you and give you directions to my house later. I gotta go," she said in a hurry and hung up.

Pam seemed overly excited about going to see some half naked men. It wasn't really my thing. I didn't understand what women got out of it, except extreme horniness and the supreme opportunity to make a fool of themselves or be made a fool of. The men that I've seen strip before usually had perfect bodies, none of which any of my past boyfriends had ever possessed. I mean some of those guys belonged in a calendar or something. For nostalgic reasons, I started to reminisce over the old broke days in college when we used to wish we could stuff one-dollar bills down the G-strings of those guys gyrating on that T-shaped stage. Since we were no longer broke, this might be fun after all.

*   *   *   *

Kaye and I rode to Pam's house in Mitchellville that evening. A limousine was leaving as we drove up slowly to the security post that surrounded the gated community.

I followed Pam's directions through the winding maze of roads that led to her street. When we pulled up to her gigantic estate, our jaws dropped. She had a six-car garage, and it looked like there were three stories. I wasn't exactly sure, but I could've sworn that I saw NFL Redskin DeAngelo Hall walking into the front door of the home just across the street. By the time I told Kaye to look over, he had already disappeared inside. I'm confident it was Mr. Hall. I'd recognize that gorgeous dude if I was wearing a blindfold and goggles in a blizzard.

*   *   *   *

When we arrived at the strip club, we could barely make our way in the door, and it wasn't even eight o'clock. I looked at Kaye who donned a huge smile as we stormed our way further into the club. Pam led, her body cutting through the various scents of perfume.

"It's about time we got out to see what D.C. has to offer," Pam beamed.

I looked around, masking my face with my hands. I wanted to just turn and leave, but more so hoped no one recognized me in this place. Kaye peered over at me and observed my frown, then nudged me hard in the ribs.

"Ow!"

"Straighten that face up, girl," she pleaded.

One guy who we took to be one of the dancers, stopped to greet Pam.

"Hey Pammie," he said, his eyes fixated daringly at her cleavage.

"Hello," Pam answered flatly, turning her attention to the bar away from him.

He blew her a kiss, blissfully eyed Kaye and me from lips to legs, and then headed toward me. I took two steps back and braced myself for whatever he was about to say or do.

"So," he started, "what's your rate?" He wrapped his arms around me and pulled me toward him. I used my arms to barricade his chest from mine. His alcohol soaked breath crept quickly up my nostrils, making me woozy.

I pushed him away and placed a hand on my hip. "*Excuse me?*" I asked.

Pam interjected, "Not that type of party, Orion. Beat it."

He rolled his eyes at Pam, and disappeared into the sea of surrounding women.

Kaye bulldozed her way over to Pam, almost flattening me in the process.

"Girl, who was that?" she yelled.

"Nobody," Pam replied. "Now let's find a better place where we can see."

Kaye rubbed her hands together greedily, as Pam led the way deeper into the abyss of lustful women. She located a nice spot with an optimal view of the dance floor where the guys would be performing.

Just as we located an empty table, music blared over the loud speaker piercing the women's chatter as the room became pitch black. Almost in unison, screams, howls and cheers commenced, as we stumbled in the direction of the vacant table. I covered my ears and tried to refocus my eyes to adapt to the dark, but it was no use. D.C.'s best male strip show was about to get underway. All I could hear was Kaye saying, "Aww shit."

A spotlight shone on this tall dark bald Adonis just rippling with muscles. The music died for a moment as the dancer leaned his frame against the opposite wall where he had just entered. He stealthily walked through the crowd. Prince's classic hit, "Do Me Baby" started playing and the noise decibel almost broke the sound barrier, while some women attempted to stand in their chairs to get an unobstructed view of this erotic god. I shook my head, giggled to myself and made a mental note of where the nearest exit was in case a riot ensued. The brother *was* fine.

Kaye leaned over to me, "I would bear his children and not *even* ask for child support."

Pam's voice became a siren as she clang her hands together loudly like cymbals. As he made his way through the crowd, the women were groping his muscles and stuffing dollars in his pants pockets.

"Damn, he didn't even dance yet!" I noted loudly.

"He doesn't need to!" Pam yelled over the music. "Do you know who that is? That's Chocolate Mocha Munch, girl."

"*Chocolate Mocha Crunch?*" I asked with a sour expression.

"Munch! Munch!" Pam corrected.

I rolled my eyes to the ceiling and shook my head in disbelief. My belly ached from laughing hard as I wiped away the tears that had accumulated in the corners of my eyes and simmered down from his outrageous stage name. 'Chocolate Mocha Munch' as he was called, spotted me in the crowd and made his way over to where we stood. Kaye was gripping and slapping my arm maniacally.

"He's coming this way!" Kaye said.

Chocolate Mocha Munch was standing face to face with me. His minty breath caressed my face as he looked deep into my eyes and licked his lips. Chocolate's cologne stringed my senses along as he leaned in slowly and softly touched my neck with his lips. The women were baying like wolves at a full moon and began chanting, "*Take it off.*" A portly woman came up behind him, slapped his rear end and tucked a bill in his back pocket, then scurried away.

I could feel my cheeks burn as he caressed my skin. I just wanted his handsome ass to go away. Well, my wish came true. He walked away all right, with a handcuffing grip that tugged me right along with him. I tried to pull away from him by playing a tug of war with my arm as I walked in the opposite direction, but Kaye and Pam shoved me back onto the dance floor. I looked back at the girls and Kaye gave me the thumbs up as she buckled over, unwilling to contain her laughter.

What was he about to do? I thought to myself as my body temperature rose to about 117 degrees.

He stood me carefully in the middle of the floor like a magician's assistant as the spotlight shone down on me. I started to tiptoe away when he turned his back, but his long arms pulled me back into position like a rope yanking a young calf at a rodeo. The legs of an old diner chair screeched across the hardwood floor as he drug it to center stage. He ordered me to sit down, but I firmly stood my ground, arms folded. He placed his hands on my shoulders like a vise and pushed me down in the seat – hard.

He leaned over and whispered in my ear, "Try to relax."

I could feel the sweat forming under my armpits with every passing moment. Prince's song ended, but another one of his classic love songs began – 'Beautiful Ones.'

He parted my legs and buried his face deep in my crotch. I looked down at his bald head and palmed it like a coconut. The women started howling as me and

Chocolate became showered in dollar bills. He put my legs on his shoulders, placed his hands firmly on my hips and lifted me up as he came to his feet. I yelped and dug my fingers deep into his hard flesh. I was so high up in the air; I thought my head was about to scrape the ceiling. He looked up at me, showing off his gleaming white teeth and high cheekbones. I looked at his bulging shoulders and tried to make out the tattoos on his arms. After inspecting his arms, I closed my eyes and silently prayed that he wouldn't drop me. He slowly squatted to the floor and laid me down carefully on my back. He spun me around like a beer bottle and tossed my legs over his shoulders. I knew that I would have to go to the store for a tube of *Ben-Gay* after all was said and done. More dollar bills showered us. He started thrusting his midsection ferociously into mine. More dollars.

I wondered if all the money was his, or if some of it belonged to me as well. After all, he was using *me* to provide entertainment for these sex-starved women. I could hardly wait until this fully clothed porn show ended.

I shielded my face with the tail of my shirt as he took my free hand and raised me to my feet. He gave me a kiss on the cheek and whispered in my ear, "It wasn't that bad was it?"

I nodded in disagreement.

He smiled and said, "If you want the real thing, it can be arranged."

"Thank you, but no thank you."

"Well, I'm sure I'll see you again. I know your friend Pam," he said with a wink of the eye.

During my walk of shame back to where I stood before I was violated, I felt a sharp slap on my behind. I leapt from the pain and saw Chocolate holding a wooden paddle like he was about to hit another homerun out of Yankee Stadium. So I doubled back, reached down and grabbed a fistful of dollars, then took off. My butt was still stinging from that slap!

*   *   *   *

We giggled in the car the entire time on the way back to Pam's. They were both talking about what they would've done had it been them with Chocolate Mocha Munch instead of me.

"Shoot, I might've flipped *him* in the air." Kaye screamed. She and Pam slapped five over the seat.

"Calm down," I interrupted their banter. "Y'all would've been just as embarrassed as I was."

"Whatever," Kaye concluded.

"Do you know what he said to me?"

They were both silently awaiting my answer to the question I'd posed to them.

"He said that the real thing could be arranged if I wanted."

Kaye, who was sitting in the passenger's seat, looked over at me in shock. *"What did I just hear you say?"* she exclaimed

"So what'd you say?" Pam asked almost simultaneously.

"What do you mean?" I defended. "I told him thank you but no thank you."

"Sula, you are so prudishly funny, girl," Pam concluded. She hopped out of the car and leaned into my window. "Kaye it was nice meeting you."

"Same here."

"Alright then," Pam said with a yawn. "You guys get home safely."

I waited until she made it securely inside and drove off.

"Do you believe the size of that house?" Kaye asked.

"It was gorgeous wasn't it?"

"Wonder what she does for a living?"

After a few minutes of silence, I noticed that Kaye was studying my profile open-mouthed with a slight smirk.

"What are you looking at, Kaye?" I said, still keeping my eyes fixed on the road.

"Chocolate Mocha Munch was trying to hook up with you?"

"Kaye, he was trying to make some extra money," I said. "I know there was a lot of money on the floor, but they *were* just dollar bills."

"So you think they prostitute on the side?"

"I don't want to speculate, but he seemed pretty comfortable asking me what he did."

I had decided earlier not to ask Pam where and how she knew Chocolate Mocha Munch. As my mind replayed flashbacks of the entire evening, I felt that I would probably be seeing him again as he claimed. My thoughts were interrupted as Kaye blurted out in raucous laughter.

"What's so funny?"

"When you grabbed the money," she gasped to catch her breath, "what were you thinking?"

"Hell, I deserved that seven dollars!"

Chapter Nine - That's Pam, from Portland

I raced into my office and almost injured myself as I slid into my seat trying to grab the phone before it stopped ringing.

"Hi Sula, this is Marla in Pittsburgh, what's going on?" she beamed.

"Well hello there, Marla in Pittsburgh!" I joked, "How's it going?"

Marla was an art dealer that I bought a lot of my prints from. Like me, she was in business for herself and had been in the art industry for over 15 years. She was highly successful and owned three homes. One of which was nestled quietly in the Bahamas. I used to ask her a lot of questions regarding the business when I first started my own gallery. We met at an art conference back when I was living in New Orleans and have been doing business off and on since I opened my gallery. She always has an inside track on the hottest prints that are in high demand, and would call me as soon as she got word.

Marla always spoke like she was in a hurry. She never wasted time with small talk – not during business. Once business was conducted, she was laid back and sociable.

"Going good, I got a nice piece for you if you're interested," she spat out.

"Oh yeah? Who's the artist?"

"Never mind that, the piece is selling like you wouldn't believe. The print goes for $15 wholesale, but I've seen other stores sell it for as much as $55." She sounded like she had just taken a bite out of an apple or something else crunchy.

"What is it?"

"A naked girl," she swallowed her food, "what else?"

"Well, I gotta see it . . ."

"Sula, have I ever steered you wrong? Trust me. I can have 500 to you by Friday. Put it on your website and get ready to order another 500. You can sell 'em for $30 to start, and then raise the price if you want. You won't have 'em long. Hold on."

My chest slowly rose and fell while I was entertained by Frank Sinatra's song, "I Did it My Way." She was making a pretty good offer, but I wanted to see the piece before I purchased it. I mean, she was talking about a $7,500 deal without sight of the product. Then again, everything that she'd sent me before sold within a month or less. The vision of failing to successfully sell this mystery piece ran through my mind like photographic snapshots in fast forward. I had to make a decision fast.

"Sorry about that," Marla said when she returned to the phone. "So what do you wanna do, Sula?"

I hammered out a rhythmic rap on my desk with my pen, bit my lower lip and stared at the base of the phone.

"Okay, give me 250 to start. I'm taking your word, but I don't want to be stuck with 500 pieces that won't sell in this market."

"I got you, girlie. I'll have 250 to you by Friday. Matter of fact, I'll even sell them to you for $10 a piece. But," she emphasized, "when you call me ready to order some more, the price is $15. I'm just warning you."

"I hear you, Marla. I'll call you Friday, when they come."

*   *   *   *

On Friday, Tara came into my office to inform me that my order from Marla had arrived. I asked her to bring it in. She dragged the box into my office and went back up front to her desk. Like a skilled surgeon, I whipped out my box cutter and opened one end of the package. When I pulled out one of the prints, it was upside down and I saw the chiseled silhouette of the naked woman as Marla had described. When I turned the print around to view it upright, I wobbled slightly and fought to regain my balance. It was Pam!

So this is how she made her fortune, I thought. Let me not jump to any conclusions. Being in this business, I know that models get paid well, but not *that* well. I wanted to let Pam know that my gallery was about to sell her print, but I didn't want to embarrass her. I had to figure out a tactful way to let her know without prying too deeply into her personal business, so I decided to invite her out to lunch that afternoon.

While I was on the train to Metro Center, ignoring the clicking of the wheels against the tracks, I tried to think of what exactly I would say to open a discussion about the artwork. I wondered about tap dancing around the subject to see if she would just break down and confess. Or should I just ask her if she'd ever posed nude before? Just before the conductor announced my stop, I had decided to just come right out and be forthcoming with all of my questions.

"Hey, Sula," she greeted.

"What's up?" She hugged me and showed me to our table.

"I got here early and got us a table."

I felt ill at ease because I had convinced myself on the walk over from the station that I would just be up front, but it was becoming more difficult now that we were face to face. My eyes gazed nervously from patron to patron as we walked single file to our table. She sat down and casually glanced toward the entrance of the restaurant. Her lips curled up slowly then formed a wide smile.

"Oh my goodness! Sula, excuse me for one second," she said, lifting up from her seat.

Pam approached this guy who was fashionably dressed; from his Italian shoes to the diamond watch on his wrist. He cradled Pam in his arms and enveloped her with a warm hug and smooch on her neck. The brother was without a doubt, attractive. I tried unsuccessfully to read their lips, and felt out right guilty for spying.

When she turned to come back to the table, I awkwardly cast my eyes downward to the menu and pretended that I was reading the contents the entire time that she was away.

"Excuse me," she apologized and sat down, "that was someone I know from L.A." She waved her hand as if he was nobody and continued eyeing the menu.

"Pam, guess what I got in the mail today?"

She looked up apprehensively, "What's that?"

"A new print that one of my dealers said was a must have."

"Oh, that's great. What's the piece called?" she asked with a smile.

"Eve's Competitor."

She slowly closed her menu and set it down on the table. She placed a cooling palm to her forehead. It trailed to her cheek as she smiled uneasily. "Well, then you know one of my little secrets. Yes, once upon a time I used to pose for a few photographers. One guy was so confident that it was a sure thing that he pitched it to an art dealer who reprinted the piece. People began buying it in droves. The demand went up and I received a nice bit of change for it. And yes, I still get residuals."

"Pam, I know what models make in this industry. I mean, a house in Mitchellville, girl?" I chuckled lightly. "What do you do for a living now? You never told me."

She tilted her head slightly as her near closed eyes locked with mine.

"Sula, can you just drop it?" she opened her menu again.

"Sorry Pam. I just thought we were becoming really great friends . . ."

Her jaws were clenched tight and her face held a look of disdain. Her voice carried more bass as the words passed her barely parted lips when she replied, "Not *that* great . . ."

"Well, excuse me for making that assumption," I responded. She sipped her water, unfolded her napkin, and placed it neatly in her lap. Reluctantly, I had decided to drop the subject even though the suspense was killing me. I couldn't think of anything else to talk about without the conversation appearing to be fake and forced. Finally, she broke the silence after a few minutes.

She started in a hushed tone as frustration and anxiety built in her voice. "Why did you have to get that stupid print of me?"

"It just kind of fell into my gallery," I quietly answered.

Her forehead was glistening from the perspiration. She rubbed her hands together nervously and cleared her throat.

"When I lived in Portland I was a stripper, okay? That money at the publishing company just wasn't cutting it. I always wanted to move, but I just couldn't make enough loot to get out of that place."

I felt like Barbara Walters as I listened intently to her story. It wasn't adding up to me. I knew she had expenses while she lived in Portland, she may have had a nice nest egg, but enough to move across country and into a million dollar home?

Pam looked in her lap, shook her head and took a deep breath. I had no idea what I was about to hear. Judging by the display of anxiety, it was obviously something that still nagged at her conscience.

"You gotta promise not to say anything, I'm not proud about it."

From the way she prefaced the news, it sounded extremely personal. I took a deep labored breath, "you've got my word."

"After I left Portland, I moved to L.A. for a little while." She looked down in her lap, "Why am I telling you this?" she asked herself out loud, eyes still focused downward. She shook her head as her sorrowful eyes met mine. Whatever it was still hurt her deeply and I immediately felt like shit for prying.

"Pam, you know what? Don't bother." I sighed empathetically, "it's really *not* my business. I just wondered about the artwork. That's all."

Pam broke down and cried before she got up and ran to the restroom. The wind from her shameful retreat brushed lightly across my face. I dropped my shoulders as my eyes became fixated on her empty chair. I pushed away from the table slowly and then got up to follow her. When I reached the ladies room, I cautiously opened the door; there wasn't anyone inside other than her in a stall crying softly.

"My God, Pam," *I* was fighting back tears by now, "I didn't mean to make you cry. I definitely didn't mean to make you drudge up any terrible memories either. Do you want . . .? Maybe I should go . . ."

"No!" she yelled. "You stand right there and listen!"

I stood frozen while she blew her nose and continued to sniffle before she began.

"When I moved to L.A., I hooked up with a Madame and became an escort. Those were some high paying clients. The money was good and I finally made enough to move. So when the time came, I left the west coast and came back east. I lived in Georgia, had a terrible short marriage with a man who was into construction more than me. He just didn't love me at all. Uh! Then I came here. The guy I was talking to just now is the Madame's son. I knew he was somewhere on the east coast, but I had no idea he was in D.C. For a while I did that *and* stripped four nights a week. I saved every penny and left the first chance I got."

She continued crying. I finally took the breath I was holding from the moment she said she was a call girl.

She busted out of the stall and pushed me out of her way before rushing over to the sink. Her hands cupped the water from the faucet and she roughly dashed her face with it. She looked up in the mirror at herself for a moment and then reached for some paper towels, but I handed her some instead.

"Pam, I'm not judging you," I reassured her. "I know how it is when you're on your own; you felt you had to do what you had to do. It's in the past."

"Yeah Sula, so many people say that," she scoffed. "The minute you saw my house I knew right then that as a hard working business woman, you were wondering how I could afford to live there and not you. So you *were* judging me. Well now you know!

"So many damn nights I dealt with groping hands, liquored up breath, stalkers, death threats from women, cheating husbands, TWO abortions . . ." she shook her head at the thought, "I earned that fucking house. I earned it! Every square foot of it! The bad part is that I feel like I may have to go right back to that lifestyle here in D.C. just to *keep* the house. And to see the Madame's son again after all this time, confirms it. Oh my God."

"Pam . . ."

"Just leave me alone, Sula!"

I stood there for a moment as my heart went out to her. It seemed as though she had to compromise her body and probably her morals just for material possessions. She had to be in some unimaginable pain. One piece of artwork that found itself in the office of my gallery had just caused her to reopen wounds that may have taken her years to heal from.

"I'm still a friend if you need one, Pam."

I walked out of the restroom and left the restaurant. I had no appetite for lunch.

Chapter Ten - Sex Interrupted

I felt like doing something special for Ray, so I invited him over for dinner and a romantic evening. The doorbell rang just after I had double-checked all of my dishes that were warming in the oven. I opened the door and Ray's eyes twinkled when he smiled to greet me. He leaned in to give me a kiss on the cheek and I invited him inside.

"You look beautiful," he said as he swung around and held out a bottle of champagne. "This is for you."

"Thanks, Ray. Have a seat." I walked in the kitchen to put the champagne on ice.

"There's a lot I want to talk to you about this evening, Sula."

"Really?" I said, while removing the contents out of the oven and placing the pans on trivets.

"Everything smells so good."

"Well, it's ready, we can eat."

"Why don't you have a seat and I'll fix our plates," he volunteered.

As I took my seat, I was instantly impressed with his consideration. Once he served the food, he sat down and took my hand.

"I'll say grace," he announced.

"Okay," I responded as we bowed our heads.

"Gracious Father, we thank you for the food that we are about to receive for nourishment and to strengthen our bodies. Thank you Lord for allowing the both of us to share a nice evening together and I pray that there will be many more to come. Amen. Oh and bless the cook 'cause it makes no difference how fine she looks."

I giggled, "Uhhh, amen."

I watched him unfold the linen napkin and place it carefully in his lap. For some strange devilish reason, that prayer of his turned my sex meter to 'full throttle' as I imagined him sweeping the table top clean of food and dishes to take me right then and there. Even the crazy "bless the cook" line.

He took a bite of his food and dropped his fork back down on the plate in a loud clatter. He sat back in the chair, tossed his head back and looked up toward the ceiling. He slowly started applauding.

"Oh my God, Sula. This salmon is five star, baby."

"Thank you. I'm glad you like it."

"No, baby, I love it."

We ate in silence for the next few bites, which I actually took as a compliment, because he was shoveling in the food. However, I decided to let him speak first.

He stopped eating for a moment as he watched my every movement and broke the silence with his milky voice.

"Sula, I want you to be my lady."

I didn't have any food or liquid in my mouth, but I almost choked. I sipped some champagne to swallow down whatever had risen in my throat.

I smiled, "the salmon must *really* be good!"

"I want us to be together. I've been thinking about you over the last few days. I just thought I'd better snatch up this amazing woman before someone else does. And I know you have to beat the brothers off of you daily," he chuckled.

"You'd be surprised," I countered. A lot of men in D.C. rarely said 'hello' let alone approached me. I didn't really understand why. Maybe they felt it was their turn to be chased because they believed there was a severely unbalanced ratio between men and women in the tri-city area – which is completely untrue. Who knows?

"So? What say ye?"

"Exclusivity?" I clarified.

He reached over, grabbed my hand and began caressing it, as he looked me deep into my eyes. I stared back wondering what he was thinking. This man was educated, successful, fine as hell, and had some common damn sense. He seemed to be perfect for me, but truthfully, I was terrified. I just couldn't take another crushing heartbreak. I had given my all in the last relationship with Lawrence, only to be disappointed. My last *serious* relationship, which was five years before

Lawrence, left me totally baffled. I still had several unanswered questions that would probably be unanswered forever, but somehow I couldn't let it go. Ray, in all of his sweetness and genuine sincerity, was my opportunity to press forward and finally forget about those unresolved issues from my past.

He rose from his seat and lifted my hand to join him. He gently pulled me toward him and kissed me. As I begin to suck on his tongue that was gently exploring my mouth, he reached up, unfastened my hair and loosened it with his fingers. He tilted his head back to look into my eyes.

Without exchanging words, he picked me up and carried me into the living room. He placed me carefully on the couch and slowly climbed on top of me. We continued kissing and groping each other passionately. I had known Ray for about four months now and didn't know where our friendship would take us.

"Sula, I want you so bad." He said as he broke the silence and wild kissing. "I want you to be with me."

"Ray . . ." I moaned and kissed him deeply as my hands massaged his muscular back. I wanted him too. This was the best moment to consummate our agreement to be together. We were taking our relationship to the next level.

Then it happened. My damn phone rang.

"Don't get it," he pleaded through muzzled kisses.

Ring!

"What if it's important?"

"But it's late."

Ring!

"Ray?" I whined as he continued to kiss me and started to undo the mandarin collar buttons on my dress.

Ring!

"Ray? Ray? Ray?! I have to answer it," I reached over and grabbed the phone from the receiver before he could object. "Hello?"

"Sula . . ."

"Vanessa?"

"Sula . . ." her voice cracked.

"Vanessa? What's wrong? Are you okay?"

"No," she went silent.

I sat up as Ray rolled over on his back and looked straight up at the ceiling.

"What is it?"

There was still no answer. I was beginning to worry what had her so distraught. Her quiet sobbing slowly became audible and erupted into an uncontrollable released frenzy of tears.

"My God, Vanessa, what is it? You're scaring me!"

Ray sat up and studied the fear on my face as he caressed my shoulder.

"Sula, I'm in the hospital."

"The hospital? For what, what happened?"

"I was in a car accident."

"An accident?! Are you alright?"

"No."

My head pounded from shutting my eyes tight to hold back the tears. "Which hospital are you at? I'm on my way."

When Ray and I arrived at the hospital, we went straight to the emergency entrance. The nurse led us to Vanessa's room.

I couldn't fight back the tears as I followed the nurse through the maze of corridors, dodging in and out of other nurses, doctors, and visitors. I didn't know what sort of condition Vanessa was in and was terrified to find out because on the entire ride over, I imagined her wrapped in bandages from head to toe. I regretted the fact that we hadn't spoken in over a month over that Kenard fiasco, as guilt found residence in my conscience.

Ray put his arm around me. "Are you going to be okay?"

I shook my head and patted his hand as it rested on my shoulder. We walked into her recovery room and it was as bad as I had thought. Her leg was in a cast and up in a sling. Her arm was tightly bandaged from the elbow down. She had a few abrasions to her face and looked as if she had lost more weight.

"Vanessa!" I broke away from Ray and hugged her carefully as she instantly began to cry.

"What on earth happened?" I started patting her hair back in place.

"Oh Sula, I'll be okay. I just can't believe this happened." She looked over in Ray's direction. "I remember you, but I forgot your name."

"Ray," I reminded her.

"Yeah, from the art exhibit. How have you been?" She tried to sit up a little and contorted her face from the pain. I patted her shoulder to convince her to relax and not over exert herself.

"I've been fine. What happened here?" Ray asked with concern as he pointed to her bandages and took a step closer to the bed.

Vanessa looked up at me, then tilted her head toward Ray and bashfully glanced downward.

"Oh uh, Ray, could you excuse us for a second?" I asked him, pleading with my eyes that I was appreciative of his support. He nodded with a slight smile and excused himself.

"Kenard was driving. Sula, he had been drinking."

I closed my eyes and my temperature began to rise. I thought about how inconsiderate he had been to Vanessa the night we all went to the Cheesecake Factory and now he had been careless with her safety. I calmed myself by taking a deep breath and let her continue with her story.

"We got into an argument over something so stupid." She reached over for a tissue and dabbed at her eyes.

"How did the accident happen?"

"Well, he got upset with me and grabbed my face. He turned it toward his and was arguing at me without watching the road. We veered into the oncoming traffic lane and were about to hit an eighteen wheeler head on."

"My God!" I placed my hand over my heart.

"I screamed and he swerved off the road and smashed into a guardrail."

"Oh, Vanessa," I started crying all over again. I had almost lost my friend over some idiotic boyfriend of hers with his drinking and driving.

"I've never been so scared before in my life. I thought about everything that I had done in my life. I had to call you, Sula. I mean, a few more moments in that lane...," she paused at the thought, "I know we aren't talking, but . . ."

"No Vanessa, it's not that we aren't talking . . . well, I guess we've both just been pretty stubborn lately." I held her hand.

"I shouldn't have shut you and Kaye out, I apologize for that. And the way I defended him at dinner. I'm sorry I spoke to you that way. I felt really bad about that."

"Well, Vanessa, I want to ask you something, but I don't want you to get upset."

"Uh huh."

"For Kenard to grab your face during an argument . . . has he ever hit you before?"

Vanessa was deathly quiet. Her eyes searched the blanket that covered the rest of her body. Terror gleamed from her eyes as if she recounted an incident, or maybe several, before her face balled up in an attempt to hold back her tears. She began to nod her head as she held the tissue close to her face.

I took a deep breath and bit my bottom lip.

"But he apologized and I forgave him for it. It's over," she sighed. "I know my car is ruined."

"He was driving *your* car? Was *he* hurt?" I asked, hoping that he was lying up in this hospital somewhere, so I could go and unplug some device he was connected to.

"I don't know. I blacked out."

"Vanessa, why is that boy hitting you?"

She remained silent and stared out at the darkness through the hospital window.

"Vanessa, I know you're in pain and I don't want to lecture you, but do you plan on continuing a relationship with this dude?"

She thought about it, and then she shrugged one shoulder.

I was speechless as I shook my head and began pacing around her bed.

"Vanessa, I *know* I know you better than this. You just rest up for now. I'm glad it wasn't much worse than it could've been."

"Me too, Sula."

I leaned over to give her a hug and she patted my back. "I'll come by to see you tomorrow. Do you need me to bring anything from home or anything at all?"

"Some decent toiletries." She chuckled lightly, "Toothpaste, deodorant, you know. Stuff like that. Are my keys over there in the drawer?"

I walked over to the little night table and opened the top drawer. Her keys were inside along with her wallet and other personal effects. I grabbed the keys and held them up.

"Got 'em."

"Do you mind going to my house to get some clothes for when I leave?"

"Okay." I patted her hair, "I'll definitely bring your comb and brush too, girl." I tried to lift her spirits with some sarcasm. It worked, but once she was about to really get into her laugh, she stopped herself because of the pain in her leg.

"Ow . . ." she answered the discomfort. "I hate the hospital."

"Sorry, it was a bad joke." I gave her a comforting smile and turned to walk out. Just then, Kenard came barging in her room and pushed me out of his way like a swinging door. Other than the white square bandage on his forehead, everything else appeared to be fine.

"Vanessa, how are you, honey?"

He leaned over and began kissing her face all over.

I wanted to take a few steps back and kick him square in the ass as if I were about to kick the winning field goal during overtime at a Super Bowl game.

"Excuse me?" I said rudely.

He turned to look at me, "May I help you?"

"Oh, Kenard, you remember Sula, don't you?"

He stood up and walked toward me, bobbing his head like he was about to be part of a rumble.

"Yeah, I remember her," he said with conviction. "Well, thanks for stopping by." He turned his back on me in an act of dismissal.

"*Kenard*?" Vanessa pointed out his rudeness.

"What? She was leaving, right?"

I balled my fist up and looked down at my shoes. I had on some pointy-toed black alligator pumps. I knew it would be painful for Kenard if I kicked him where I wanted to, but I restrained myself. Instead, I looked frantically around the room for something to clobber him with. When I couldn't find anything, I glanced back down at my shoes. I pulled one off and held it up with the heel facing outward and started toward him. I felt someone grab my hand and spin me around to the room's exit. I looked up at the hand that gripped mine and then at the person who had just saved Kenard's life.

"What are you doing, young lady?" the voice said and carted me out of the room.

"Ray! I was about to go upside that fool's head." I continued limping in the direction he was pulling me.

"Why? What's going on?"

"That idiot was the cause of the accident! He was drinking! Ray, I swear, if anything happens to Vanessa because of him . . ."

"I know, I know. Let's get you home." He continued to hold on to me, restraining me from going back to her room. He released me just long enough for me to put on my shoe. Once I had slipped it on, he pulled me in the direction of the exit.

"I'm glad you answered your phone, Sula."

Chapter Eleven - I Hate the Hospital

As Kaye, Pam and I made our way to Vanessa's hospital room, I quietly prayed that Kenard would *not* be there. I remembered how he and Kaye didn't hit it off at all.

"Hey!? Disabled person!?" Kaye joked as she bent over to hug Vanessa.

Vanessa was sipping on a can of apple juice when we came in. She smiled behind the straw, then set the can down and began laughing.

"You ain't right, Kaye."

"Vanessa, I want you to meet Pam. We used to work together when I lived out in Portland. Pam, this is Vanessa," I explained.

"Hi. Sorry it's not under better circumstances," Vanessa apologized.

"Well, it's better than not meeting at all. Sorry about your accident. I hope you recover quickly," Pam told her.

"That's nice, Pam. I think I like you better than Kaye," Vanessa teased.

"Alright, you keep it up, I'm gonna turn one of these switches to *off*," Kaye said as she lightly tapped Vanessa's arm. "So how long are you gonna be in here?"

"Well, they have to run some more tests and will be monitoring me closely for the next few days. I'll probably be leaving by Friday."

"Where's *Kenard*?" I asked with a hint of content.

"He left a few hours ago. He said he would be back, but I'm not sure when."

"Well, I hope we roll out before he gets back," Kaye said. "You know he almost got sucker punched the last time we were all together."

"I could never forget," Vanessa sighed.

I looked out of her window in a daze as the girls talked. Vanessa had interrupted my thoughts to find out what had me so engrossed.

"You okay, Sula?"

I turned to look at them before speaking.

"Vanessa, what is it about this dude? I mean, you seem hooked."

"Sula, despite this incident, he's good to me. You just don't know."

"Come on, girl. He didn't like any of us the first time he met us. Then when I came by yesterday, he damn near knocked me down."

"He did *what*?" Kaye asked.

"Sula, you're doing it again."

"Doing what?"

"You're trying to make me live by your ideals!" Vanessa announced.

Pam folded her arms in front of her and eyed me devilishly.

I walked around to the other side of the bed and could not believe this scathing that I was hearing. It seemed apparent to me that if Vanessa's relationship with Kenard continued, she would either be in the hospital more often, become his punching bag or wind up inside of a body bag.

"Vanessa, I don't want you to live by my ideals. I just want you to know that you deserve better. Don't you get it?"

"I know he's not Mr. Perfect or Mr. Owns-his-own-business like Ray, but he's all I got. If you haven't noticed, no one is trying to sweep me off my feet. Not like you'd understand." She reached over and grabbed a Kleenex.

I stood with my jaw slacked as Kaye scoffed and shook her head.

"I do," Pam chimed in softly and uncrossed her arms. "I know we just met Vanessa, but Sula *is* right. It's a road to nowhere, trust me, I know."

Vanessa dabbed at her eyes with the tissue before she spoke.

"I've tried to leave him," she said almost inaudibly. My eyes met Vanessa's tear soaked ones. "I can't. He won't let me."

"What do you mean, *let you?*" Kaye nearly yelled.

"You've tried to break up with him before?" I asked.

"Twice. He got so upset one time . . ." she blurted out her pain and fury in a low steady cry that broke up to indicate how many pieces her heart had shattered into. "I told him to get his things and get out. He took me by my shoulders and shook me. He said *he* would decide when it was over."

"Vanessa??" Kaye said with fire in her voice, "Why didn't you tell us!?"

"I feel like I'm losing myself," Vanessa spoke the words into the fistful of tissues she had pressed against her face. "I know if I just do what he says it will be okay from now on..."

"No. We've gotta get you some help. This can't keep up," I told her.

Just then, a young redheaded nurse who looked about 16 entered.

"Okay ladies. I have to administer some medicine to Miss Vanessa. It will make her pretty drowsy."

"That's a nice way of saying 'get out'," Kaye said as she headed toward the door.

"No problem, nurse. Come on y'all," I pulled Pam along.

We started on our way out the door with me in the back of the line. I turned to look at Vanessa as she mouthed the words, 'thank you'.

Vanessa's fear overshadowed her inner cries for help. It seemed her situation was more serious than I initially imagined when I saw them together yesterday. Now, I had to be careful. I did not want to put her in jeopardy with Kenard, but I needed to help her.

"Excuse me, miss?" a tenor voice said that echoed in the hallway.

We all turned in unison toward the person who called out.

"You dropped this," the man said as he handed Kaye a slip of paper. He was a little taller than Kaye, had a tan complexion, short hair, and a baby face, with dark thick eyebrows. He looked as if he was no more than 21, but he had to be older, he was wearing a doctor's uniform.

"Why, thank you," Kaye accepted the paper without looking at it. Instead, she and the doctor stared dreamily into each other's eyes. I looked around the corridor because I was sure to see some short, chubby man with wings standing off in the distance viewing the targets he had just struck with his arrows. Incredible. I've never seen the actual moment of love at first sight this close up. It was…well, to say the least…sickening.

"What's your name?" he asked.

"Kaye," she smiled slightly.

"Kaye. I'm Michael. My friends call me Mike."

"Michael. Like the angel?"

He smiled and nodded, "I'll take that compliment."

"Well, *Dr.* Michael," she slyly pried, "I've got to go." She turned and began to walk away. Now this was a true mack move. Kaye threw out the bait and teased him like a fisherman waiting to reel in a 30-pound mackerel.

Kaye knew men liked the chase and always made them pursue her.

"Uh, hold on!" He took a few quick steps to catch up with her. Pam and I were, of course, a few paces ahead watching this player in action. Kaye, not Michael.

"Yes?" She turned and flipped her hair all in one exaggerated motion.

"I hope I'm not out of line, but I'd like to take you out to lunch sometime soon. Can I give you my number?"

"Lunch sounds very nice."

"Okay, you have my card already."

Kaye looked puzzled, and then looked at the paper he said she dropped. She looked up at him, smiled and gave a soft nod. He pulled out a pen from the breast pocket of his starched gleaming white jacket and wrote something on the back of it.

"Call me at home if you can't reach me here at the hospital."

"Already giving orders?" she teased.

"Doctor's orders."

Kaye blushed at the comment and smiled, "Nice meeting you Dr. Michael."

"The pleasure is all mine."

Kaye turned to walk toward us and of course, being the pro that she was, she added more wiggle to her walk. *Years*, I thought, *years of practice were all revealed in less than five minutes.*

Michael was still watching her walk away and Kaye never looked back. With that small exchange, I could tell Michael was already hooked.

"You lucky devil," Pam patted her on the back. "Do you know how many times I've prayed to walk into a hospital and come out with a fine doctor's number? You go girl."

"Yeah," she sighed, "it's a blessing and a curse."

Chapter Twelve - Kaye's Match

I had a bit of extra time that afternoon, so I decided to meet Kaye downtown for lunch at this place that served various noodle dishes. Even though the restaurant smelled like all of the paper cups and take out boxes that they stored in the back were on fire, the food was pretty good. We decided to sit outside and enjoy the last few days of the warm weather before the temperatures would soon yo-yo during the month of September.

"Did you call the doctor yet?" I asked Kaye as I spooled a wad of noodles onto my fork.

"Not yet."

"Why are you waiting?

"It's just been two days. I'll call him this evening," she slurped up a few noodles and giggled. "Did you see how he looked at me?"

"I saw how you looked at *him*."

"And how was that?"

"You had big red hearts for eyes, girl. I want you to call me after you talk to the doctor."

"No way. Our conversation will be classified. You already know too much of my damn business as it is!" she barked.

"Not only am I your bestie, I have a need to know, so that declassifies your classified information. Therefore, I'm privy to the sordid details," I giggled and she laughed at my silliness.

"No you need to figure out who guy number three is. Didn't that blind woman say three guys?"

"Yeah, she did. I don't think I need the third one. They would have to really out do, Ray," I told her. "But for real talk to me after you talk to the doc!"

I hadn't talked to Kaye in a week.

In the meantime, I spoke to a few police officers about Vanessa's situation and they said that they couldn't do anything because there was no crime. They suggested a restraining order and left it at that – so much for protecting and serving. I called a few women's shelters to see if they had any suggestions at all. They offered her a room at the shelter, but the waiting list was estimated to be a year. They also suggested that she move or stay with friends. That was easier said than done.

Fortunately, Vanessa hadn't seen or heard from Kenard since she'd been home. She joked and said that it was probably because his transportation, her car, was no longer available. Maybe there wouldn't be a need to switch residences.

It was Thursday night around eight and I was not about to leave straight from work and go home. I felt like going to a happy hour somewhere nearby to unwind. Since Vanessa was recovering and Kaye was probably out and about with the doc, I called up Pam. She agreed to meet me for a drink and some appetizers.

It seemed as though every nine to fiver was at this happy hour. The music was thumping and the line was quickly forming on 17th street. I remember when there was never a line at this place. Maybe there was new management in place. On Thursday's they had all night drink specials and karaoke, which was an interesting combination. If laughter was food for the soul, I knew my soul would be well fed by the drunken talent this evening.

"Hey, what's up?" Pam asked when she met up with me.

"This place is packed!"

"Packed with men!" she beamed.

Pam was scouting the venue for someone, anyone. She was checking out every man that walked past us -- the tall ones, the short ones, the stocky ones and the old ones. She was not about to discriminate when it came to sinking her hooks into one of these fellas.

"Are you horny or something?" I asked her. She looked at me as if I told her that the building was on fire and we needed to evacuate.

"What? Why'd you ask me that?"

"Because you're looking at *every* Tom, *Dick* and Harry that's walking by. What's up with you?"

"Well, I won't lie. I'm looking to fornicate a bit tonight."

"Well, there are plenty of guys here, so you won't have to look far."

Just as I said that, she grabbed this guy's hand as he walked by us. He was a cute dark-skinned brother with thin shoulder length locks. He had on a beige button down shirt that looked like it was made from burlap. The shirt was opened just enough to see the top of his muscular chest. He stopped when he felt someone restrain him. When he saw that it was Pam who had held him up, he began to smile.

"Hello there," she said.

"Hi," he replied. "Did you want to dance? Why'd you stop me?" He smiled and awaited her answer, and so did I.

"No I don't want to dance. I want to . . ." she leaned toward him and whispered in his ear. His smile was so wide, that it seemed the corners of his mouth had met his earlobes.

"Your friend too?" he asked.

Pam looked at me and then shrugged. "I'll ask her." She leaned over to me, but I immediately put my palm in her face.

"You don't have to ask me nothing. You know I don't get down like that." I rolled my eyes at the both of them. Something *told* me to just roll out here to happy hour by myself. I mean, I knew from what Pam told me about her past that she had probably done everything under the sexual umbrella, and I preferred to be left out of whatever it was that she whispered in that dude's ear.

When I had basically denied Pam the opportunity to hear her agenda for the night, he shrugged and told her that he would be back in a minute.

"What's up with you?" she asked me defensively.

"What do you mean?"

"You're not down for having any fun?"

"Excuse me, but people die years later from "fun". Girl, please. You don't even know that dude."

"I know, but isn't it great being a woman though? You can get free sex whenever you want it!"

"Okay, you're scaring me," as I slightly turned away from her.

"Feel me on this one for a minute. Woman can go months and months without sex, by choice, and then if we decide, hey, I want some ding-a-ling and hope he blows my back out, all you have to do is walk out of your front door!"

"And right into the door of a clinic."

Just as I said that, Kaye tapped me on the shoulder.

"Kaye!"

"Girl, I know I've been quiet, but you know how it is," she summated, and then shrugged.

"Umm hmm. And just where *is* your doctor?"

"Hey Pam!" Kaye ignored my question.

"What's up, girl? Sula almost missed out on a ménage a trois."

"What???" Kaye held her mouth open as she looked at me in disbelief.

"No, Sula *did* miss out on a ménage a trois. Pam's horny ass is over here recruiting brothers," I defended. "Anyway . . . your doctor?"

Michael walked up behind Kaye and kissed her on her exposed shoulder, then smiled at us.

"Hey babe," she responded to his affection. "Mike, you remember my girls from the hospital. This is my ace boon, Sula and her friend, Pam."

"Hello again," he said with an accompanying million dollar smile.

"What's up, Doc?" I said just to be corny and I started laughing. "I always wanted a reason to say that. I couldn't resist."

Mike blushed, chuckled, and then looked at Kaye. Kaye shook her head and placed her finger in her throat as if she was going to gag herself.

"How long have you ladies been here?" he asked us as he hugged Kaye closer to him.

"Oh I would say about . . ." I started, but Pam rudely overlapped my statement.

"We just got here. So, what kind of doctor are you?" she continued.

"Internal medicine."

"Ooo, I like the sound of that," Pam flirted. "So you know all about how the body . . . ticks?"

Kaye gave me a look that slightly masked her anger. I knew that Kaye wasn't going to sit by and let this blatant flirtation on Pam's part continue. If I didn't come up with some excuse to separate those two, I think Kaye would've reached over and snatched all the hair off of Pam's head, as if it were some cheap wig.

"That's exactly right," Mike responded as if Pam were a reporter with Black Enterprise magazine.

"I've had some pain in a few areas," Pam informed him. "Maybe I need to come see you."

Kaye shifted slowly from one leg to the next and shot Pam a look that could've turned her to a pillar of salt right where she stood. Just as I saw Kaye fixing her mouth to respond to their little exchange in banter, I pretended as if something exciting was going on at the entrance of the establishment that would divert Pam's attention long enough for Kaye and Mike to depart.

"Oh snap!" I yelled over them, "there's Kanye West!!"

"Girl, where?!" Pam screeched as she stretched her neck to peer over the patrons to get a glimpse of nothing.

"There!" I pulled her along toward the front door, and looked over my shoulder at Kaye and waved good-bye. She gave me a thumbs-up sign and carted Mike off to the rear of the club.

When we approached the doorman, Pam was highly disappointed.

"Excuse me," she asked the doorman rudely, "but where is Kanye West?"

"How the hell should I know?" he responded.

Pam looked at me awaiting an explanation.

"I could've sworn I saw him. Must be the strobe lights," I shrugged. I looked back in the direction that we just came from and saw that Kaye and Mike had found a table in the back of the room. Despite Pam's slightly disrespectful comments, Kaye and Mike appeared happy as they began to converse with one another.

*   *   *   *

"So, are you having a nice time?" Mike asked.

"I am," Kaye responded.

"What was up with your girl? Why was she flirting?"

"Because you're handsome," Kaye smiled, "but I'm not worried about her. She was clearly out of line, but my girl Sula fixed the situation."

"How long have you and Sula been friends?"

"Since college. About 13 years I guess."

"Kaye, I just wanted to say that I've had a really nice time with you this past week. I've got a good feeling about you," Mike smiled and sipped his club soda just before he began to look deep into Kaye's eyes.

"You do?" she smiled.

"Yep. I just hope that the age thing doesn't bother you."

"I'm just a few hours older than you," she winked at him. "Okay, about 17,000 hours. So you're 28 and well ahead of the game."

"How so?"

"You're already well into your career, which is in a great field, you graduated top of the class and you know that you plan to open your own practice within the next four years. You're on the right track. Not to mention you've met yourself a fabulous woman," she teased him by brushing up against his arm.

He lifted his arm to put it around her shoulder and hugged her close.

"You're right about that."

Kaye only knew the surface of this man, but sensed that his soul was bottomless. She wanted to explore it all and be captivated more than she was currently. She was prepared to be open to receive him completely.

As they continued their getting-to-know each other session, the disc jockey announced the first karaoke singer for the evening. It was Pam singing a Whitney Houston song from the Bodyguard soundtrack, which was probably one of the most difficult songs for anyone other than Whitney to sing, "I Will Always Love You."

As soon as Pam began singing, the crowd began to talk quietly amongst themselves. The further along she got into the song, the louder the talking had become. She was, without a doubt, one of the worst singers to hold a microphone that obviously starved attention.

"She needs to politely place the mike back on the stand and tip toe back to her seat," Mike said. Kaye laughed and smiled bashfully at Mike. Kaye's favorite past time was talking about people and Mike won points with the well constructed verbal zinger for Pam. He caressed her cheek as Pam belted out another revolting riff. Kaye gave Pam's singing a thumbs down.

"She's moving like she needs to scratch something in a special place. I can prescribe something for that," Mike explained.

Kaye leaned over with laughter after taking in his comment. She peered up front at Pam as she strained to get out the notes that were impossible for her range. The crowd became agitated, for good reason, and slowly began booing. Some people were imitating the Showtime at the Apollo siren in hopes that someone would drag her off stage. Unfortunately, "Sand Man" also known as Apollo's terrible talent ouster, wasn't available for duty, so the crowd would have to grin and bear it. It was obvious that Pam was going to finish the damn song.

"If I had a tomato, I'd throw it at her," Kaye said. Mike laughed so loud at her comment that the people around them, turned to look and laughed along with him, even though they didn't hear Kaye's wisecrack.

At that moment Pam finished murdering the song, the crowd cheered because she had stopped hurting their ears. Kaye and Mike looked in each other's eyes, touched foreheads, and shared a sensuous kiss.

Chapter Thirteen - Back in Town Again

I stepped out of the shower, dripping wet after I'd realized that I didn't have a towel nearby. Stepping on a cold bare floor with wet feet, felt like walking barefoot on a sheet of ice. I was already running a little late and was glad that I had picked out an outfit to wear the evening before. I wanted everything about this night to be special.

I had already turned the ringer off on my home and cell phone. I wasn't about to chance having any interruptions. Not to mention I had already given all of my girls a stern warning not to call me at all tonight.

"Wow, you look great, baby," Ray exclaimed as he stood on the porch taking in every inch of me from top to bottom.

"Thank you! Come on in."

He gave me a peck on the lips just before crossing the threshold and came inside.

"You ready?" he asked.

"Ready? Uh oh, what's on your mind?" I nudged him.

He paused for a second and grinned, "To go out. What's on your mind? Ooo-weee! We can stay in if you want," he raised his eyebrows up and down quickly and reached for my waist. I playfully backed away and laughed.

"Later! You should eat first, you're gonna need that energy," I playfully scorned and winked at him seductively. "I'll grab my purse."

*   *   *   *

We hopped in his car and started toward the Waterfront.

"We're going dancing? I have the wrong shoes on," I curiously informed him as we turned in the direction of one of the nightclubs whose neon lights were flashing off and on to entice people in the vicinity to come inside.

He laughed at me and placed his hand on my thigh, then gave a gentle squeeze.

"Just hold on, sweetie," he said as he wheeled the car onto Water Street.

After he parked it in the garage, we headed upstairs. It was a little cool for a late September evening, but the warmth of his arm wrapped around me shielded the gentle wind.

"Where are we going, baby?" I asked, suspense taking a strong hold of me.

"The Odyssey, for dinner and dancing."

I gasped and took in as much air as my lungs could hold before I looked up at him and smiled wide. He pulled me close to him as he squeezed my shoulder. Then I felt his soft lips plant a moist kiss on my forehead as we made our way to the dock.

Once we boarded, the hostess took us to our table and announced that we would be setting sail in approximately fifteen minutes. She poured us both a glass of white wine and left us to talk to one another over the candlelight.

"How long had you been planning this?" I asked.

"I've got my secrets. You like it?"

"I love it. This is so romantic, Ray."

"Go ahead and say it. I'm the man . . ." he smiled and held his chin up awaiting my declaration.

"You the man," I said pointing both fingers toward him. "So how was your business trip?"

"No, no, no, no, no. We're not talking about work tonight. We're talking about you and us."

"Me?"

"Yeah, you."

"And us?

"Sure, why not?" He sipped his wine and beckoned the waiter over.

Once the waiter took our orders, Ray looked over at me with a colossal smile, eyes twinkling from the candlelight.

"What?" I asked in regard to his gazing.

"Tell me, Sula. What are you expecting from me?"

"Ray, in my infinite wisdom, I've learned to expect nothing."

His shoulders rose and fell as he sighed. "Come on, Sula, be for real. Tell me and be honest."

"Okay," I started, "a fear of God, trust, sincerity, consideration, love . . ."

"Alright alright, let me stop you right there. Tell me something that isn't on a laundry list that you want from me, not men in general."

"Well," I sipped my wine and thought long and hard before I spoke. "You seem confident to me. But there are situations where art buyers aren't looking for art. They pretend to be interested in art just to talk to me. I need for you to trust that I've been doing this long enough to know the difference."

"Sounds fair," he said.

"Observe me enough to know when I'm having a down day and be proactive. Even when you may not feel like it. I'd do that for you."

"Sounds special," he sipped his wine.

An announcement was made over the intercom that we were about to set sail along the Potomac River. The dancing would begin right after dinner was concluded. A violinist made his way to our table and graced us with some exquisite sounds. The cruise was breathtaking because our dinner table had an unobstructed view of the river, Northern Virginia and D.C.'s skyline. Ray sipped his wine and stared into my eyes as if he had something that he desperately wanted to say.

"What's on your mind, hon?" I asked.

"Your beautiful brown eyes, girl." He shook his head slowly as he closed his eyes and savored whatever he was imagining. "They're so hypnotic."

I blushed and traced the rim of my champagne glass delicately with my fingertip.

"So, Sula Mae . . ."

"Yes, Ray?"

"Could you see yourself settling down with someone like me?"

I took a moment to take in what he had just said. Ray's comment had totally caught me off guard; we'd only known each other for about five months. I thought his line of questioning was a little premature, but maybe some men didn't feel the need to dawdle when and if they knew what they wanted.

"Ray, you're a sweet guy. You're hard working, responsible. You have so many qualities that I've always wanted a mate to possess. From what I know, I would say yes."

"You like kids?"

"I love kids. They are silly, brutally honest and funny to me."

"That's good to know, Sula. With so much going for you, why weren't you snatched up a long time ago?"

"Well, timing is everything," I nervously cleared my throat as I tried not to choke on the words that just passed my lips. I dabbed the corners of my mouth with my napkin, and stared for a moment at the residue of dinner that was on the china plate. I forced a smile and continued, "Apparently, it's never been the time." I folded my napkin and placed it beside my plate.

"You ever been in love?"

I took a deep breath and a dramatic pause before I looked at Ray with a doe-eyed expression. "Yes. I have."

"What happened?"

"It was a while ago. It's kind of difficult to talk about because I don't know what happened to him."

"You still love him?"

"Honestly, I do think about him at times, but only because there was never any closure. It's hard. I feel like I'm being held hostage, but maybe I'm holding him hostage. I don't know Ray. I feel odd discussing this with you. I'm really glad that you're a part of my life now. I've had no choice but to let go because you've taken up so much space in my heart now. I don't want to sound cheesy, but it's like you rescued me."

Ray looked deep into my eyes with seriousness overwhelming his face. He held his hand out for me to take it, which I did. He placed his lips against the back of my hand and kissed it. He held his lips there for several seconds before he rose from the table. "Come on, let's dance."

The small band played some contemporary music and we danced close. After Ray and I danced for one tune, he looked at the live band, shook his head and screwed up his face in distaste.

"Nah, nah, I need some music where we can get down like we did when we first met. 'Member that?" he smiled and continued swaying back and forth to the music as my body molded into his like a puzzle piece.

"How could I forget? A tall lean brother doing the penguin was a sight."

He threw his head back and laughed at the mere remembrance. "Yeah, but you were looking pretty sexy doing the snake. Mmph."

I shoved his shoulder at his remark.

"Body moving like a silk scarf in the wind. I was like, 'who is this beautiful woman moving like *this*?'"

"Cut it out, Ray!"

"No really, I saw you when you first came in."

"Really?"

"Yeah. You moved around the club so much that night, it was hard keeping track of you. But when I saw you later, I wasn't gonna let you get away from me that easy. You were definitely the finest woman in the spot. I'm glad I caught up with you finally."

"Me too, Ray. That night, you were making me laugh so hard and I really needed that. You just don't know. That won some serious cool points with me."

"Oh, you like it when I make you laugh, huh?"

"Yes, baby I do."

"I think I can do that for the next fifty years."

We stopped dancing in the middle of the floor, as I looked deep into his eyes. He stared in mine, never blinking as he looked at me seriously and intently. As I became lost in his eyes my body temperature rose slowly as my heart pumped quickly. I accepted his comment and kissed him seductively on the lips. He wrapped his arms around me and pulled me close to him. I felt his strong arms caress my back in an up and down motion as my body began to melt.

After we kissed, we stood there looking into each other's eyes, speechless. I didn't realize that we were the only ones on the dance floor as the musicians played. For a moment, it seemed as if we were the only people on the entire cruise. I cleared my throat and nervously smiled. My body was tingling all over as if tiny electric shocks were being administered to my nerve endings. He smiled his signature pearly-toothed smile and escorted me off of the floor.

We walked to the upper deck to peer out over the water and said nothing. His body was pressed firmly against my back as his arms cradled me from behind. I tilted my head backward and let it rest on the curve of his neck. Safety was what I felt as we stood there in complete silence, enjoying each other and allowing ourselves to think in peace. I tried not to let my mind go into overdrive because of his comment. Instead, I calmed myself and reaffirmed what I told him earlier. *Expect nothing.* It seemed like a negative comment as I looked out over the river. Perhaps I should have been telling myself, *'expect everything, you deserve it'.*

Once we docked, we hopped in the car and headed back to his place.

A thousand and one questions raced through my mind as I previewed what the evening would be like. Will he like my body? Will he be pleased with me? Will *he* please me? What will sex with him be like? Will it be awkward afterward? Will he call me first the next day? What will he think if I call him first? I took a deep breath and let out a huge audible sigh.

"You okay?" he asked.

"To be honest. I'm nervous."

"Me too. But it will be fine. I know that tonight is our night. As long as none of your friends call," he winked at me then looked back at the road.

"I know why *I'm* nervous. Why are you nervous?"

"Well, Sula, it's been a while."

"How long?" I inquired as if I were a detective.

"Just . . . a while."

"Longer than sixth months?" I asked with a slight drawl in my tone. It was as if I had forgotten what sex was like. I watched Ray out of the corner of my eye, and to my surprise he was smiling. "What are you smiling about, Ray?"

"Six months? I'm impressed. I know you've had several offers."

"What's makes you think I've had several offers?"

"Sula, you're fine, okay?"

"You're embarrassing me!"

"I'm not trying to, sweetie, but come on. How many numbers do you throw away in a day, huh?"

"None. I call 'em all!" I laughed. "No really, I waited because I wanted something special."

                    *   *   *   *

When we arrived to his place, there was champagne chilling in what used to be ice and a mink throw on the floor in front of his mahogany coffee table. On the table, there was a fondue set, and boxed chocolate.

"Kick off your shoes and take a seat on the floor. I'll be back."

I did as instructed and inspected the box of chocolate to pass the brief time. Ray came from the kitchen with a huge tray of strawberries that were on steroids.

"Ooo, chocolate covered strawberries," I clapped to show my enthusiasm.

He chuckled as he set the berries in front of me. They smelled so sweet that I wanted to dig into them as soon as the platter hit the table. Ray turned on some Anthony Hamilton and prepared to do a mock strip tease as he took off his suit jacket. I giggled and watched his tall, dark and handsome frame show off. I was so turned on as I watched him move seductively, and wondered what he was going to do to my body.

He fed me strawberries and sipped his champagne. I fed him a few berries in between kisses.

"I almost forgot. I got something for you."

"What?" I set my champagne glass down and looked up at him as he stood before me smiling cynically.

"I almost didn't get it, but I wanted to see what it looked like on you."

"What is it?"

He stepped out of the room and returned with a small box wrapped in silver paper with a blue ribbon tied around it.

"What is this?" I asked again as I shook the contents of the box.

"Open it."

Being careful not to tear the wrapping paper too badly, I opened the box, and inside was a beautiful white gold cuff bracelet. It had to have been two inches wide.

"Ray, this is lovely!"

"Can you try it on for me?"

"Sure!" I hesitated at first then had a bright idea. I did not anticipate doing a strip tease for him but what better way to model the bracelet? I was nervous, but decided to show myself off to him anyway. If we were in a monogamous relationship, he was bound to see me sooner or later.

I placed the cuff on my left wrist, walked over to him and turned my back. I looked over my shoulder and down at him with a sensuous smile.

"Will you undo me, please?"

He stood with a grin masking his face and slowly unzipped my dress. As he unzipped, his fingertip caressed my back causing it to arch from the sensation. I turned to face him and paused for a moment. He carefully took his seat back on the throw and watched me as if a life saving surgery was being performed.

I raised my left hand to my right shoulder and in an exaggerated motion to show off the cuff, began to pull my dress down my arm. I did the same for the opposite shoulder and slid out of my dress – shifting one side to the next over my hips in a seesaw motion. His eyes caressed my body like a warm bath as he gazed at my neck. His eyes then began moving slowly down to my breasts that were hidden behind the blue brassiere. I stepped out of my dress revealing the matching thong and stood there before him. He gazed at me for several seconds without saying a word. He just wore a sly grin. I wondered what he was thinking. It seemed as if he were secretly plotting his sexual attack against me.

"You're wearing my favorite color, you sexy thing you."

"You like?" I asked giddily as I wiggled my hips.

"Mmm. Can you turn around for me?"

I took a deep breath and slowly rotated myself around. When I turned back around to look in his face, it had contorted as if he were in pain. However, I knew what that look meant. Almost every man I had known, seen or heard of, makes that face that translates into a single word to express their extreme pleasure with the way a woman looked – "*Damn!*"

I threw my head back and giggled. He stood up and approached me stealthily. He kissed my lips, softly, then my shoulders.

"You smell so good," he said through muted kisses.

As I kissed his neck and face, I felt around his chest and stomach and began to undo his shirt. Once I exposed his shoulder, I kissed it delicately giving it gentle bites between kisses. I nestled my mouth at the curve of his neck and continued kissing. He gave a low moan and rested his hands on my hips. He slowly slid his hands to my waist and gave a single squeeze. I looked in his eyes and caressed the trench of his back gently. He looked at my mouth and breathed his hot breath onto my face. He took a quick nibble on my bottom lip, and then lapped his tongue in one quick stroke across my mouth.

He lifted me up and carted me off to his bedroom. He tossed me on the bed and damn near ripped his pants off before he joined me. He straddled my body and cupped my breasts, then digging his fingertips into my flesh, he ran his hands down my rib cage, waist, and to my hips. I looked into his eyes as he licked his lips and blew me a kiss.

"Thank you for my gift, sweetie," I told him in my sexy airy voice.

"Did you read the engraved message?"

I took off the cuff and focused my eyes in the muted light to view it. *Be mine and I'll be thine.*

"Oh Ray...," I said with a moan.

My eyes, like the soft candlelight in the room, bounced around Ray's body from muscle to muscle at the vision set before me. Our eyes met for a moment. As he slowly began to smile, I broke contact, only to gaze at his single dimple being formed, and the curtain of his perfect teeth.

"I waited so long for this, Sula," he said to me. "I'm going to please you like you deserve to be pleased."

And he did – all night long.

Chapter Fourteen - The Big 3-0

In three days, I will be thirty years old. When I was 18, I mapped out my entire future. Long ago, I was interested in pursuing a career in law. I would be receiving my J.D. by the time I turned 25, and opening my own practice at 27. I would marry someone that I had met in law school by 26 and have my first child at 28 or 29. I was going to have a son first and name him Jordan. My next child, a daughter, was to be born two or three years after Jordan. Her name would be Amaria. Our nuclear family would live in a two-story home with a pool in the backyard; there would be a fireplace, two car garage, picket fence, blah blah blah . . .

That perfect calculation for my life's course, or so I thought at the time, had shifted like a piece of property on the San Andreas Fault line. Although I was happy with the way some things were in my life, I had begun to take an inventory of the goals unaccomplished by age 30. I had set so many goals for myself, with a slightly skewed realistic approach to the time factors allotted for each. The single most problem with me now, as opposed to ten years ago, was I wanted things too fast. This must come with turning 30, because in my twenties, I felt as though I had all the time in the world. That's what I get for taking it easy for 10 years.

I don't think of myself as a failure at 30 by any means. I have made some significant moves toward my future. Instead of harping over what I didn't accomplish over the past decade, I would use the *next* decade to settle the score. Having the successful continuation of my art gallery for the next decade and thereafter is number one. I spoke with my neighbor in the strip mall where my store is located and found that he's going to be moving. His property will be for sale and I'm seriously considering investing my money to expand my shop. I'll be calling my real estate agent this week. How about *that* for the first item of business in my thirties?

Who am I kidding?

I'm not looking forward to it in the next three days! I've seen this day of elderliness coming for the past 362 days and three more days does *not* make a difference. Last week I went to a nearby park to clear my head for a few minutes and meditate on my life's numbers rotating to 30, like those numbers on the old-fashioned gasoline pumps . . . how depressing. Hell, I was already settling in to old age. I was sitting on a park bench!

The morning of my birthday when my alarm went off, I laid in bed listening to its loud sharp beeps. For a moment, I thought I was listening to a heart monitor in a hospital room. I clicked off the alarm as my eyes remained fixed on the ceiling for about five minutes as I debated whether or not to go in to work.

As I sat up and swung my feet out of bed and onto the floor, I had a terrible pain in my temples. I squeezed my eyes as tight as I could to subdue the ache and prayed for it to leave quickly. When it finally subsided, I stood up. The noise my body made once I arose, frightened me. It sounded like firecrackers exploding in all of my joints. I frowned at the resonance and slowly slid my feet across the floor as I prepared to go to the art gallery.

I turned on the faucet for the shower and set the water temperature as hot as my body could withstand. I looked in the mirror at my reflection for a few moments to see if I noticed anything different. I wiped the redness away from my eyes and tried to get a better look.

"What is that?" I said aloud as I peered closely at my reflection. I looked up at my hair and stretched my neck closer to the mirror. I squinted my eyes while my fingertips gently parted my hair. A long strand of gray hair! This single strand was as white as a snowcapped mountain in Colorado. I couldn't believe that I hadn't noticed it growing before today. Or perhaps just yesterday, this strand decided to turn white for precedence sake.

I wanted to yank it out, but an old wives tale revealed that if one gray hair was pulled out from the scalp, two would return in its place. In that case, so much for a quick cosmetic fix to my aging process. I wondered what else I would discover today. It would probably be gray hairs growing in my ears or something similarly unappealing. Before I started to pick my appearance apart any further, the phone rang.

"Hello?" I answered groggily.

"Happy birthday, sweetheart!"

"Thank you, Ray," I didn't sound very enthusiastic and he picked up on my low-keyed spirit. I wasn't sure at that hour if it were the affects of being a year older, or if I just wasn't fully awake.

"I wanted to be the first to wish you a happy birthday. You're going to work today, right?"

"Yeah," I moaned.

"What's wrong, love?"

"Other than hearing my body sound like a trash compactor this morning and finding a gray hair, I'm okay."

He started laughing. "Sula, you are something else, baby. At least your birthday landed on a Friday. Besides, turning 30 is not that bad."

"Oh yeah?"

"Yeah. In fact, I bet this day will get better as it goes on. You'll see. Oh, what time is that party tonight?"

"It starts at eight."

"Okay. What are you doing for lunch?"

"Probably taking a bottle of Geritol, then having my cholesterol checked," I joked quietly. "After the diaper of course."

"You silly, baby," he teased, "I'll drop off your hearing aid and Grecian formula."

I believed Ray when he said that the day would get better. By the time I had pulled into the parking lot where my gallery was located, I possessed quite a euphoric feeling. When I walked inside, Gayle and Tara were already there. I stopped in the doorway and to my surprise; these girls had decorated the entrance to my office in the rear. Amidst the several black balloons, that led the way, there was a huge black banner with silver lettering hanging over my office door that said, 'Happy Birthday, Sula'. There were cobwebs that dangled from it and miniature coffins. At the foot of my office doorway was an opened paper coffin maybe 2'x2'. A skeleton lay inside surrounded by jars of Icy Hot, Doan's pills, Metamucil and Tums. Tara had a cane leaning against her desk with a sign pinned to it that said, "Sula's." After I took in all of the old and decrepit motifs surrounding my birthday, I smiled and shook my head.

"Happy Birthday!" they both yelled.

"I've just got two things to say. One, these decorations had better be for Halloween. And two, I hope you didn't use any petty cash for this!" I laughed, gave them a hug and thanked them for their thoughtfulness.

"Well, go to your office and put your briefcase down and give us some work to do," Gayle said as she gave me a little shove toward my office.

"What are you two up to?" I asked suspiciously.

"You have any work for us?" Tara asked again.

"I'm not giving you two any work, because after today, y'all are so fired."

I walked away shaking my head at their antics. Before walking into my office, the smell of fresh cut flowers collided with my nostrils. I flicked on the light switch and screamed.

"Oh my God!" I looked around with the hugest grin my mouth has ever made.

There were red, pink, white and peach roses – balloons in almost every color. I felt tears well up in my eyes as I looked at the huge poster board seated in my chair. It read, 'Happy Birthday, My Heart.'

"Ray!"

Tara and Gayle came into my office and studied my face for its reaction. I tried to hold in the tears but I couldn't. This was by far one of the nicest things any man has ever done for me.

"When were these delivered? I don't understand," I questioned while smelling the yellow roses.

"Ray called us last week," Tara confessed. "We told him that we would be here last night to decorate the office. The roses came last night and the balloons were here first thing this morning. He instructed us to be here by seven."

"Say, are we gonna get paid extra for doing all of this?" Gayle teased.

*   *   *   *

I closed the gallery at four to go home and prepare for the party.

By six thirty Kaye and Vanessa came by my house so we could all ride together. Ray was going to meet me there so we could leave together. My heart went out to Vanessa as she hobbled in my house. She stood on her crutches and gave me a one armed hug so she wouldn't lose her balance.

"Happy Birthday, Sula!" she cried.

"Aww, 'Nessa. Thank you, but why are you crying?" I asked as I consoled her.

"You've always been there for me and I appreciate it. I could've handled that whole Lawrence and Kenard thing differently."

"Yeah, you could've," Kaye said, spoiling the sentimental mood. She smiled and winked at Vanessa indicating that she was joking with her.

"It's over, forget it," I reassured her as I shoved Kaye.

"So, I'll get a chance to meet this new doctor boyfriend of yours, huh?" Vanessa asked Kaye.

"Yep. He said he would meet me once his shift was over. Did Sula tell you what Ray did for her this morning?"

"Yes, I thought that was so sweet," Vanessa squealed. "This one sounds like a keeper."

"Yeah, he does," I agreed.

"I just hope that he's not the 'too-good-to-be-true' type," Kaye sighed. "Those are the ones with *major* issues."

"Nobody's perfect," I stated.

"He sounds pretty perfect to me," Vanessa exalted.

"Look, I'm not about to put this guy on some pedestal," I told them. "He's a man. It's less of a shock if things are put into their proper perspective."

"I say enjoy it while it lasts," Vanessa proclaimed. "There are some rotten apples out there. Case and point." She held up one of her crutches as an example, "but there are also some pretty decent ones on the other end of that spectrum. I just think Sula was able to grab one of 'em."

"And I hope I grabbed the other!" Kaye joked.

*   *   *   *

When we arrived at Pam's, there were barely any parking spaces available. I was beginning to think that this party was more for Pam than me. Then again, she did mention having a housewarming slash birthday sort of shindig. As we were walking up the driveway, the front door opened and Pam stepped outside wearing Capri pants and a shell shirt with a neck scarf. She had on huge sunglasses, despite the lack of sunlight. In one hand, she held a huge cognac glass filled halfway with some exotic mixture. She reminded me of Mrs. Thurston Howell, III from Gilligan's Island.

"Hello ladies," she slurred slightly, "glad you girls could make it."

"I smell that barbeque," Vanessa noted.

"Yeah girl, there's plenty of food, drinks, and the d.j. is mixing it up something fierce in there. Sula, your surprise will be here around 10:30. So I hope you rested," she giggled and put her free arm around me and escorted me into the house.

When we entered, the d.j. boomed over the microphone, "There's the birthday girl, Sula Tyler! Show her some looooove!"

These people didn't know me. If these were Pam's neighbors and other high rollers, I was relieved that I stuffed a stack of business cards in my bag. I always turned social events into networking opportunities, and this, in my opinion, was the motherload.

"Go on 'round back and get something to eat," Pam ordered. "I'll take 'Crutch' out back with me and introduce her to some folks." Pam carefully escorted Vanessa out to the deck.

Ray peered inside around the door and started smiling when he spotted me. He looked at me, winked and mouthed the words "Happy Birthday." I blew him a kiss and walked over to thank him for the flowers and balloons.

There was something about Ray that made me tingle all over. It wasn't just about our sexual experience, which was incredible, but I liked his essence. He had an aura that was hard to explain, but it gave off a positive vibe. It was like things were fitting together for once. I couldn't wait to have a dance with him and have some one on one time with him after the party.

As I crossed the room, I saw Mike come in through the front door. He closed it and stood against it observing everyone like it was his first time interacting with earthlings.

"Hey Mike!" I waved.

"Sula! Wow look at you. Happy Birthday," he said and gave me a light peck on the cheek. "Is Kaye here?"

I nodded with a smile.

"Okay, well, I'll try to find her. Nice seeing you again." Mike patted Ray on the back just before he sped off to try and find Kaye.

"Ray!" I said and planted a wet juicy kiss on his lips, "I've been waiting to do that all day."

"Oh yeah? Is that it?" he pulled my body close to his. I shook my head and gave him another kiss.

"Dance with me," I said as I pulled him away.

As we meandered through the crowd and found a comfortable spot to dance, I put my arms around his neck and looked into his eyes.

"How is your day?" he said.

"Good, but much better now," I confessed as I gently squeezed his back. I stopped dancing and grinned. He mirrored my expression, but he squint his eyes and tilted his head to one side.

"You want to go upstairs for a minute?" he asked me.

Without me saying a word, Ray gripped my hand and yanked me into the direction of the staircase. We both ran all the way to the top of the stairs and located an open and rather spacious bathroom.

"Ray!" I said in disbelief as I looked around at the bathroom. It looked like it was just photographed for an article in Architectural Digest.

He kissed me wildly as he slammed the door shut behind him and locked it. He lifted my top, moved away my lacey brassiere and kissed my chest frantically. I looked down at him and rolled my eyes upward with pleasure. The vision would stick with me for days. He sat me down on the edge of the tub and knelt down in front of me. He tugged at my low-rise pants for me to remove them. Once my pants and panties were freed, he carefully dined downtown as I tried to resist the urge to climax. There wasn't anything to support my back, so I just leaned backward and placed my hands on the base of the tub to support me.

He lifted me back upright and madly fished around in his pockets for a condom. He was succumbing to the urge to be inside of me. Once he prepped himself for a quick session, he sat on the closed lid of the toilet and beckoned me over for me to sit on top of him. He met each of my movements with precision. After a few moments, he reached around to grip my bottom and lifted me up and down rapidly like a power hammer. I couldn't contain myself any longer. I gripped his back, threw my head back and let out a long loud moan.

Happy Birthday to me!

*   *   *   *

After our quickie, we returned downstairs and most of the people had come inside and adjourned to the party room in the basement. There was a pool table, air hockey table, and a foosball game, which I never had the inclination to learn or play. A full service bar was along the wall by the pool table equipped with a large female bartender.

When we walked into the basement, I noticed the crowd had grown from when I first arrived making me wonder exactly how long Ray and I were upstairs. There was a single chair against the wall with balloons and streamers tied to it. Pam saw Ray and me descending the stairs and rushed over to the both of us. She had a microphone in her hand.

"Soooo," she started with her mouth close to the microphone, "what were the two lovebirds doing upstairs all by themselves?" she announced loudly.

Everyone started 'oo-ing' and 'ah-ing' as if they were sixth graders and the lights were just turned off in the auditorium. I felt as if I had a sign on that said, "Just had sex." Pam put her arm around me and totally cut Ray off with her shoulder. She escorted me to the chair and started to make another announcement. I felt like I was in the center ring at a circus.

"Sula, I have a great surprise for you! Chocolate Mocha Munch is here!" she boomed in the mike. The women began cheering. I looked around at everyone baffled and wished that she would put that damn microphone down. You would've thought she was a CNN correspondent with that thing. "You've had an encounter with him before if I recall, and he brought two of his good friends with him! Thunder and Mystic Reign!"

I reached for the mike and struggled to pull it toward me, "No! No! No *encounters*! None!"

I hardly classified seeing the negro dance as an encounter.

The music blared loudly and I looked over at Ray. He wielded a confused expression. I'm sure the word "encounter" rung out with him as well. He folded his arms in front of him and leaned against the wall. To make matters worse, Chocolate Mocha Munch gave me a firm pop on the rump, causing the crowd to whoop and holler. I turned in his direction as I tried to console my stinging ass and glared at him. *Not here*, I thought.

Chocolate Mocha Munch approached me even closer, wearing black leather chaps and a black cowboy hat. He looked scrumptious as hell, and I tried desperately not to admire his goods, which was difficult. The men were shaking their heads laughing and checking out all of the horny females in the place. I had no idea Pam was going to do this. As fine as Mocha was, I thought about how I would feel if some exotic Amazon was shaking her stuff all in Ray's face. Once that image played in my mind, I moved away from Chocolate Mocha Munch before he had his stuff in mine.

I saw Vanessa standing off in the corner and rushed over to her. I grabbed her hand and helped her hobble over to Mocha. She was trying not to be forced to sit down, but she also had a huge grin plastered on her face. The crowd murmured and chuckled when they saw a temporarily crippled lady making her way to the seat. I knew that Mocha wouldn't be tossing some woman on crutches in the air. Besides, Vanessa didn't make our outing that night and this would be my way of letting her know what she missed.

Vanessa took her seat as I took her crutches and placed them against the wall next to her. I walked over to Ray and tried to make him smile by making a funny face. He looked deep into my eyes and planted a moist kiss to my forehead. He shook his head and placed a firm hand around my waist. It was amazing to see the number of stunts that Mocha pulled off with a woman who had a full cast on her leg. I don't think he improvised, I was sure he'd done it before!

*   *   *   *

By the time I was gathering my gifts together, Pam's house was still packed. I guess they were competing to see who could empty Pam's liquor stash the fastest. Pam came over to help me with the gifts.

"I had planned those men for *you*," she scorned.

"I know girl, but my man is here. That wouldn't have been cool," I retorted.

"Is he *that* insecure?"

"That has nothing to do with it, Pam," I corrected her with an accompanying shove.

Ray came over to us and stood by me as he looked at the gifts. He clapped his hands and then rubbed them together. He had been whispering clues in my ear all night about what else he had for me and wanted to do to me, so I'm sure he was anxious to leave to get the second party started.

"You almost ready?" he asked happily.

"Yeah, just grab her things and I'll walk you guys out," Pam commanded before walking away. She grabbed some items and headed for the door.

Vanessa was off in a corner talking to Mocha Munch. She waved her crutch at me as I was heading out.

Kaye grabbed the rest of the things and we made our way outside to Ray's car.

"Is that everything?" Ray asked jovially with a single clap of his hands.

"Yes," Pam answered flatly, "if she missed anything, I'll be sure and drop it off to her."

"Thanks for the party, Pam. I appreciate you doing that for my baby," Ray gave Pam a handshake and opened the car door for me to get in.

"Anytime," she replied. Pam eyed his hyper activeness strangely by creasing her eyebrows and slightly shaking her head with disgust, but Ray didn't pay her any attention.

"Kaye?" Ray said to her, "Take care of the doc. He seems pretty cool."

"Thanks Ray, I will. You take care of my Sula," Kaye instructed him.

Ray scoffed, "I thought you had something hard for me to do." He smiled and began to load the packages in the trunk. I turned to face Pam.

"Thanks for the party," I hugged her and looked at Kaye over Pam's shoulder. She lifted her fingers to her ear and mouthed the words "call me." She began pumping the air with her midsection quickly before Ray caught her in the act. I fanned her foolishness with an unconcerned hand and got in the car.

"Well, Sula, happy birthday boo boo!" Kaye innocently sounded once her gyrations ceased. "Let me go in here and get Vanessa. I think she's still talking to that Chocolate Peppermint dude."

Once I drove off, I looked over at Ray and he returned my glance with a smile. He patted my leg and gave it a tender squeeze.

"Now we can finish what we started earlier," he sexily announced as he rubbed my leg up and down. "Did you enjoy yourself?"

"It was a bit of alright," I responded contently.

"I just wanted to tell you, that was a really nice thing you did in there tonight," he looked in his rearview mirror then peeked over at me.

"What did I do?" I asked.

"You got up, put Vanessa in the chair for the strippers, came and stood by your man. Ummph. That was some sexy shit there. You made me feel really special," he paused as he slowly approached the stoplight. He turned in his seat to face me and placed his hand on my cheek. "I love you for doing that and I'm gonna make sweet love to you all night."

Chapter Fifteen - Searching for Sula

I was working on yet another Sula original painting. I had studied so many techniques and had seen so many types of art; I figured it was high time that I focused more on creating my own in addition to selling other folks work. Besides, it was a great outlet and gave me the chance to get away from any and everything for a moment. Just as I was rinsing my paint brush, there was a knock on the frame of my office door. I looked up and couldn't believe my eyes.

Like a heavenly vision, there stood a tall man with a dozen pink roses garnished with baby's breath shielding his face. I had no idea who it was. I set down my paint pallet and tried to make an educated guess as to whom it could be. Ray was in Seattle, so it wasn't him. I hadn't heard from Pedro since the hallway dilemma and Lawrence was clearly absent and gay. I was clueless as to who this could be; all of the men that I didn't romantically hit it off with were abruptly cut off the following day.

"Excuse me, sir, are you in the right office?" I asked suspiciously.

"Sula Tyler?" the voice said.

When I heard the heavy Barry White-like voice, my mouth became as dry as a maple leaf floating around in the Sahara desert. I didn't know whether to be happy or angry. My first reaction was happy, then, after the events surrounding our separation played in fast forward, my blood started to boil. Here, in my office doorway stood my first true love. We spent nights, days, holidays and every waking moment together while we were in college. We talked about becoming engaged at graduation, and then getting married two years after that. His plan was to get down on one knee in front of both sets of parents and every *other* graduate's parents, and ask for my hand in marriage.

The only problem was that he didn't make it to graduation. I had never heard anything from him since then. I thought the most terrible thoughts about what had happened to him. Maybe he had been in a terrible accident on his way to the ceremony. Perhaps the night before, he was partying and got into a fatal fight with someone. The list went on and on. Now, here he stood – in my office doorway, less than six feet away from me, popping back into my life almost six years later.

He dropped the roses slightly downward to reveal those beautiful eyes that had the power to hypnotize me into submission. He moved the roses further down his face to unveil the widest grin, and the sexiest lips God had ever granted to a man in this lifetime. His face showed maturity, but he still looked young. His toasted brown complexion was still flawless.

Although his Kid 'n' Play flattop was gone, his new style was a low Caesar fade, which fit him perfectly. The ripples of waves were almost laid in unison, row by row. His dark blue double-breasted suit hung gallantly on his frame and I could see his pectorals peeking through the silk button down that was nestled behind the dark curtain of blue. He had been working out. His frame was lean in school, but he had bulked up nicely. I looked at his hands. No rings. Here stood my love, my main heart's joy, the man who was the perfect candidate to father my children and be my life's mate. Gerrard Stiles. I didn't need that African bracelet for this one.

"Hi baby," he said.

Slowly I rose from the art stool, my mouth still opened slightly as I waited for words to ooze out without a command from my brain. It was everything that I had dreamed of. That one day, he would come back to me and we would pick up where we left off. It had been five years. After a year of hearing nothing from him, I reluctantly gave the dream up.

"Gerrard?" I uttered almost inaudibly.

"Yes, Sula. It's me."

Thud!

All of my senses left my body. I distinctly remember looking into his eyes, then upward toward the fluorescent lights, but that was it. I saw nothing but darkness as I lay there on the floor.

*   *   *   *

"Sula? Sula? Suuuuulaaa?" this voice sang out.

In an attempt to refocus, I blinked my eyes several times. When I came to, I was lying on the couch in my office and could feel someone patting my hand and calling my name over and over.

"There she is," he said. I could hear the smile in his voice. "You okay, baby?"

I sat up and he immediately shoved a paper cup filled with water in my face. I turned my head slightly and sat up straight. I rubbed my aching hip and looked into his twinkling eyes. He smiled and looked deep into my lazy ones, while I blinked harder this time. It was Gerrard all right.

Almost in a reflex, I took my hand and smacked the side of his face as hard as I could.

"Hey! What was that for?" he rubbed his cheek as his smile instantly left.

I placed my hands gently on both sides of his face and planted the deepest kiss on his alluring mouth. He wrapped his arms around me and gently massaged my back with his fingertips. Then he pulled me closer, as we began to let loose years of passion. I hadn't realized how much I still had feelings for him, because after all these years the special place that was reserved in my heart just for him had completely overflowed and filled it entirely.

"No, no, wait wait," I softly ordered as I pushed him slightly away. "Is it really you? Gerrard?

What...what happened? I didn't know what happened to you. How did you find me? What happened!?"

"Sula, the night before graduation, my grandmother was rushed to the hospital. She had a severe heart attack. The next day, she passed away. She wanted to be buried in Georgia and we left to be with the rest of the family right after to make her arrangements. After the funeral, I went back to the dorms, but I was too late.

"I wrote letters, but they all came back. Did you guys move?"

"Yeah, actually my parents did," I whispered. I studied his face, I was still in disbelief.

"Then I contacted the school . . . they wouldn't give me any of your information."

He stroked my cheek as I sighed and gripped his hand in mine.

"Well, after all of this time baby, we're together. Michael McBryde is a friend of mine. You featured him at an event a while ago. He could not stop talking about the art gallery, the event, and the people this wonderful woman exposed him to. When he said Tyler Fine Art Gallery, I had to ask the first name of the owner. When he said, "Sula" – I just couldn't believe it. I asked him if he had your card and sure enough, there was your name, address and phone. I tied up some loose ends in Georgia and came up to see you as soon as I could. I know I took a huge risk coming, not knowing if you were married, had children or what have you, but I had to see you again, Sula. I just had to."

"Gerrard, it's nice to see you and know you're safe, but . . ." I started, but his words ran over mine.

"I didn't expect to get slapped, but I guess I understand. I just watched you for a moment working on your painting. You are still fuckin' gorgeous," he bashfully chuckled. "I don't know if you have plans this evening, but I made reservations at B. Smith's. Join me so we can catch up."

"My God, Gerrard, this isn't real . . . I mean, I can't believe you're here." I was still shaking and my heart was getting a thorough work out.

"You're not married but still kept your maiden name, are you?" he asked with a tinge of fear in his voice.

"No."

"Kids?"

"No. You?"

"No."

"You married?" I asked.

He took a long pause and looked down. *I knew it*, I thought.

"I've been divorced for a while now. Seven months after we got married, we were calling it quits."

He reached in his suit jacket and pulled out his wallet. In it, he extracted a tattered photo that had been folded. The photo was from our junior year when we went to Six Flags Fiesta in San Antonio. When I saw it, I laughed so hard because we looked so young and reckless. I instantly remembered that day and smiled from the inside out.

"My God, I can't believe you still have this!" Staring at the photo, I studied every line and curve.

"I kept this with me all the time. I can't believe I found you! I knew you would be successful. I just *knew* it. You had so much drive and ambition. Sula, Sula. It's really you."

"So umm, what do you do all the way down in Georgia?"

"I own my own construction company. Ranked number three in the state."

"Get outta here!" I shoved his arm. "I'm so happy for you, Gerrard!"

"Thanks. It was tough at the beginning, but once we landed some decent contracts, and the housing boom took off, it was worth it. Twelve offices and two thousand employees."

I looked over at the wall clock. It read three o'clock.

"Oh goodness!!" I yelped. "I've got a three thirty appointment with the owner of a framing company!"

"Oh sorry, baby. Dinner at seven? B. Smith's?" his eyes pleaded and I nodded. "Great!" he kissed me and hugged me close.

*   *   *   *

The valet drove my car away as I stepped into Union Station. It had been a while since I'd eaten there. The only thing I remembered was this dish called "Swamp Thing", which tasted a trillion times better than it sounded. It was delicious. When I stepped inside, Gerrard was at the bar, but faced the door. He smiled the instant I spotted him and rose to greet me.

"Hey there," he said with a warm hug. "You look absolutely gorgeous."

"Thank you. You're looking very dapper yourself." I giggled.

"Thank you." He placed his hand gently on my back and held his other hand out ahead of us. "Our table is just this way."

The hostess smiled and led us to the table. He held the chair out for me and then took a seat while the hostess poured us two glasses of iced water and told us of the specials for the evening.

"Sula, part of me never thought that I would ever see you again. This is fate. Have you tried to find me?"

I adopted a long pause before I spoke. I had exhausted every avenue and always came up empty.

"Gerrard, it took me a long time to come to grips that you were gone. I tried. My mind thought the absolute worst. As the days passed, I was sure that the worst happened. I just gave up hope. I had a new emotion everyday when it came to you. I remember your mother was from Louisiana. I moved there, hoping maybe I would just bump into you. Georgia never crossed my mind. But I guess that was all part of God's plan. New Orleans was where I first learned the inner workings of an art gallery, and decided that I would own my own, which coincidentally brought us together years later."

"You've grown so much, Sula," he reached for my hand. We softly held each other's hands over the tabletop – his thumb caressing the back of mine. "You like it here?"

"Yeah, I do. There's a lot to do here, the business is booming. My girls are here. It's great."

"You ever consider Georgia?"

My heart skipped a beat as I reached for my glass. The cold water felt like a lump of ice as I gulped it down to calm me. I shrugged my shoulders in response.

"You would love it," he gave my hand a reassuring pat. "So, how come these D.C. idiots haven't snatched you up yet? What's their problem?"

I laughed at first and then quieted down as a flashback of Ray's winning smile popped into my head. He was far from a blithering idiot.

"I don't know. I used to wonder the same thing. But I guess everything happens for a reason."

He caressed his chin, tilted his head slightly and smiled at me. I opened the menu and scanned it. In my peripheral, I could see that he was still watching me. Not only that, I could feel his eyes outline my face.

"Sula, I still love you. I've never stopped."

I could feel the tears filling my eyes and about to stream down my face as I looked through blurred vision at Gerrard.

"I will always love you, Gerrard. I just . . ."

"Sula, after seeing you this afternoon, I realized what was missing in my life. I'm glad you still love me. I *did* understand the slap and the fainting," he chuckled.

"Oh, let's not relive that."

"How's your hip by the way?"

"I took a nice hot bath and its better."

"After we eat, you want to go for a walk?"

*   *   *   *

As we caught up, and reminisced over old times, we shared a hearty laugh as we both relived the first time we met.

We were both in the campus bookstore to purchase books for our classes. As I was thumbing through the Intro to Art History textbook, I noticed someone that kept walking back and forth on the ends of the aisle. I never saw his face, only his figure. Every time I looked up to catch a glimpse of the person who was obviously lost, I would only see the rear of his backpack as he passed. What happened next was definitely planned.

I had concluded my perusal of the texts and headed up toward the register. Just as I reached the end of the aisle, BAM! We collided and books flew everywhere. He apologized profusely and picked up the scattered remains of the collision from the ground. I stood there, upset and silently labeled him a klutz, as he started snooping through my selections. He put on some phony act about being into art, but I knew better. I grabbed my books from him, gave him a weak 'thank you' and headed toward the register.

However, he wasn't going to let me off quite that easy. As I was in line waiting for my turn to pay up, I heard someone repeatedly clearing his or her throat behind me. I continued to face front and tried to ignore the incessant noise of rattling mucus. It wasn't until the person went into a hacking cough that I turned around. It was Gerrard, just like I thought. As soon as I turned around he ceased the act, waved and smiled at me. I flashed a hand, turned back toward the front of the line, and shook my head, annoyed with his disturbance of the peace.

"Good thing you're not a pre-med student," he said as he tapped me on the shoulder. "I'd be dead."

I turned my head slightly to give him a cue to leave me be. But to no avail, he kept right on talking. He asked me if I were an artist, if I majored in art and if I stayed on campus. He kept right on talking and asking me questions – loud.

I felt sorry for him after someone further back in line spoke up and said, "Jesus, will you shut up? You're making everybody sick." If that wasn't bad enough, everyone else in line chimed in with an agreeing, "Yeah!"

After that bookstore encounter, I didn't see him until a week later.

*   *   *   *

"Do you know how much suffering you put me through until I saw you again?" he reminded me. "I *knew* you were mean when you didn't even help me pick those books up."

Gerrard and I drove down to the Martin Luther King, Jr. Memorial and walked around for a bit. It was a little chilly, but I didn't mind. I was reading some of MLK's famous quotes that were immortalized in stone when Gerrard turned me around and planted a deep kiss on my lips. He pulled me closer into him and began kissing and tenderly sucking on my neck. I melted right there.

I wanted to let myself go and succumb to his advances right there in the courtyard of the memorial. Instead, he led me back to his car, walking closely behind me with his hands resting on my waist. I could feel his massiveness throbbing against my rear as we walked swiftly to the vehicle. After he opened the door for me and waited for me to sit down, he lightly jogged to the driver's side and hopped in the seat.

He reclined his seat and reached over for me. He continued to kiss me wildly as his hands explored every part of my body like they used to. I return his affection, but my wrist was restricted. I paused for a moment and slipped off the cuff bracelet Ray had given me and tossed it into my opened purse in the back seat.

"Sula, after all this time, you still drive me crazy."

He kissed my face all over and down to my neck. He ravished my shoulders gently with his hot mouth and released several short moans to soundtrack his passion.

Something felt off. His touch used to drive me absolutely insane, but not anymore. This was what I had been waiting for I thought, after all of this time. I couldn't understand why my body didn't respond the same. I had to stop him.

"Gerrard?" I quietly murmured. When he didn't respond and continued kissing and groping, I called his name again, but a bit louder, "Gerrard!"

"Huh? Yes, baby?"

"I'm sorry, but I can't do this."

"You want to go to my hotel room instead? There's a sunken tub, king sized bed, very spacious," he suggested.

"No honey, I can't do this period. I need to get home."

"Is it me? I've missed you so much baby. Please don't do this," he pleaded.

"Now that I know you're okay after all this time, I'm okay with that. But," I started as I clumsily reorganized my clothes, "I can't. There is uh . . . there's someone else."

"Oh no, Sula. No. There can't be!" he tightly squeezed his eyes shut and threw his head backward against the headrest. "I didn't just come here to see you and have sex with you. Sula, I want you to come back to Georgia with me."

Chapter Sixteen - That old feeling

Gerrard would not be leaving D.C. until Monday morning and Ray was scheduled to be back in town tonight. I hardly felt like playing a juggling game with these two men, but the little devil on my shoulder kept whispering to me to have a final fling with Gerrard before saying goodbye - that Ray would never know. But I knew that it would eat me up inside holding on to that kind of a secret. Ray talked about the idea of us growing old together just a few weeks ago. Why did Gerrard come back now? If he came back immediately after I returned from Africa, there would be no question. However in that scenario, I wouldn't want to move to Georgia necessarily because my business was here in D.C. Gerrard was not going to let me go again that easily. I know him. So that means that while he is still here, I may have some tactical planning to do for the next two days – that meant lying.

After I left Gerrard, I came home and couldn't decide whether or not to put on the Masaai bracelet. I didn't think I needed it, but the old woman did say three men. So far there had only been two. I knew Gerrard from so long ago before though, so to me he didn't count. Just for the sake of following the old woman's instructions, I put it on anyway.

That night, I couldn't get a wink of sleep.

It was all so surreal. Sometimes I'd be in a meeting and I'd zone out because I thought about Gerrard and what may have happened to him. I would flashback to the fun times we had or the silly things he would do to make me laugh, then I'd get a bit sad. But now, I know he's physically well, he's doing financially well, he's still fine as hell, he's free, so why am I not excited? Ray is a good man for me. I've waited for him too. But I don't know him as well as I know Gerrard. Maybe I should be with someone familiar instead of risking the possibility of Ray and I not working out for the long term. With Gerrard I know he loves me. This is what I've been wanting. I stayed up all night tossing over the unknown.

I was expected to be at the airport by one that afternoon to pick up "my boyfriend". It had been a week since I'd been with Ray and I knew one of the first things he'd want to do is have sex. Would years of built up passion for Gerrard be thrashed on to Ray? Would Ray notice if something were different and would he mention it? I had never been in this predicament before and had no idea how to handle it, so I needed to call on an expert for some advice before I saw Ray. It was almost four in the morning, but I didn't care. Besides I needed to get this off my conscience and get some sleep.

"Kaye? I'm sorry to wake you, it's Sula."

"You know what time it is?" she grumbled.

"I'm sorry, but I've got a situation here . . ."

I could hear Mike coughing in the background.

"Sula, if you care anything for me, you'd call me back once the sun has fully risen. Please . . ." she begged with a harsh throaty sound in her voice and then hung up on me.

"Hello?"

I hung up the telephone and tried to make myself go to sleep by keeping my eyes closed and getting into my favorite sleeping position, which was the fetal position. I set the alarm on my cell phone to ring at 11 a.m. By then, I should be rested and ready to get myself together to pick up Ray.

Shortly after lying back down, I drifted off into sleep. It was a deep sleep that put my spirit into another dimension. From above and through the clouds, I saw rolling green hills, valleys, snow capped mountains and crystal blue lakes. It was a magnificent journey and a sight to behold. In the midst of all of the spectacular scenery, there sat a house. It looked like a miniature castle, but had the warmth and feel of a cottage. I pushed open the heavy maple door and crept inside. The stony cold floor chilled my bare feet. A symphony of crackling sounds from the fireplace tucked away behind a chiseled brick opening in the corner of the room was in session. My body was a welcome mat for the warmth from the fireplace as it bathed my feet, my ankles and on up to my legs. I could hear two voices, almost in a whisper as I walked further into this cottage. As I rounded the corner of the dismal home, I saw a huge oak carved table that looked like a piece of furniture from an old fairy tale like *Jack and the Beanstalk*. Sitting on one side of the table was Ray and across from him sat Gerrard. Both men were wearing black hooded monastery robes and gazed in my direction as I entered. After my eyes met theirs, they both, in one synchronized motion, put on their hoods and bowed their heads as they faced each other.

Riiiiingggg!

I woke up; unaware of where I was for a moment. I looked up at the wall clock. It was a little after 11. I looked over at the frantically ringing cell phone and turned its alarm off. After taking a relaxing deep breath, I rubbed my eyes and sat up to gather my senses before making my way to the bathroom.

As I started toward the bathroom on what seemed like a mile hike, my home phone rang. I back tracked my steps, and answered.

"Hello?"

"Hey, sweetheart!"

"Ray? You back already?"

"No sugar, I'm at the airport about to leave Seattle. I probably won't be in D.C. until around four, babe. There were delays and I had to take a later flight. Pissed me off. I'm ready to get back and see my honey, ya know?"

"I know, I miss you too," I felt like a sack of garbage after I said that.

"What'd you do last night?" He asked with a yawn. It was eight in the morning for him.

"Went out to eat."

"I called a few times. You had me worried."

I twisted my body around to scratch a spot in the middle of my back that was nagging me at the moment.

"Didn't mean to. I'm safe, Ray."

"I know. Uh, Sula?"

"Yes?" I turned on the faucet to the tub for a bubble bath.

"There's something that's very important that I need to discuss with you when I get back in town," his voice went an octave deeper as the seriousness enveloped his tone.

"What is it?" I asked with concern.

"I'll tell you when I see you. Can you be at the airport by four, sweetie?"

I sighed, "Of course, honey. I'll see you. Have a safe trip."

I hung up. Now Ray knows better. He knows how much I hate that. I wish he'd either told me what was on his mind or just not have said anything at all. Now it will be embedded in the back of my brain until I see him later this afternoon. It was bad enough that I'm sorting through my guilt and to top it off, he's giving me something else to wrestle with. I could feel at least four new gray hairs sprouting from my scalp. I had stripped down and prepared for the milk bath to absorb deep into my skin.

My cell rang, while I was bathing so I checked the message later. It was Gerrard. He wanted to meet up for lunch. I knew there was more that needed to be said so I decided to meet him. I didn't want lunch to run past three, so I was checking my wristwatch periodically and mentally calculating how much time would be needed to say my goodbyes to him, drive to the airport and be there for Ray by four. Gerrard sensed that I was pre-occupied with something and spoke on it.

"It was nice seeing you last night, but I still can't get over the fact that you're with someone else," he told me. "I mean, I expected you to be, but I kinda wished you weren't."

I was silent as I gave a soft single nod of the head. I turned my attention to the photograph of fall that the window was freeze-framing, as my chest heaved up and down.

"Sula? What's on your mind love?"

"My boyfriend," I told him gently. "I have to pick him up in a few."

He sat back in his chair and his once joyful expression turned to stone, like a portrait that captured his angst. I started taking quick short breaths to pace the flow of my words, which I chose carefully. I parted my lips to begin speaking, but he interrupted me with a silencing palm.

"How long have you guys been dating?" he asked.

"About seven months now."

"Seven months?" he scoffed, "That's the amount of time when I knew my marriage was over. Is it serious? In seven months? How long have you known me?"

I took a deep breath this time and the vision of the dream became clear to me. The two men had me in common and I had disrespected them both in some way. That was why they covered their heads and wouldn't look at me.

"Things with he and I have been going really well. Then you show up and . . . it's confusing things for me. Of course I've known you longer, but for years I didn't. You got married, so I must not have been that heavily on your mind."

"Sula, I only got married 'cause I wanted to feel that closeness. She wasn't you and that was why it didn't work. But I found you. I want you back and I'm not giving you up for someone you've only known for seven months."

I didn't want the task of deciding between the two. I have very strong feelings for Ray, but obviously based on the history that Gerrard and I share, there must still be something there. It was not as pronounced as the fire and infatuation that once was, but it could be reignited. Thoughts of he and I were what kept me up half of the night.

Gerrard continued to sit back with his arms folded while he waited for me to continue. I tried to muster more words amongst the silence. This was clearly not my forte.

"Oh," he began as he reached inside his jacket pocket, "you left this in the car." With a slightly pouted mouth, he handed me the cuff bracelet.

"Oh my God! Thank you!" I immediately put it on my wrist and breathed deeply.

He looked slightly upset when he saw how relieved I was to have the bracelet. After it was secured on my wrist, I cupped it gently with my other hand and sighed again before I spoke.

"Gerrard, I still love you. I'm not gonna deny that. But for the last several years, I had no idea where you were or even *if* you were. You understand?"

"Yeah. I understand you're not a risk taker anymore," he told me harshly. He kept his arms folded and continued to wait for a logical explanation as to why we couldn't pick up where we left off several years ago.

"I don't know how to explain it, Gerrard. I should've told you about Ray before we went to dinner, but . . . I was so surprised to see you after all this time. The only time to tell you was, you know, in the car."

"Sula, what type of game are you playing?"

"What?" I questioned with disbelief.

"If you were that much in love with your man, we wouldn't have even made it back to my car. Don't you understand that I love you? I need you, sweetheart. Listen, I really want you to come to Georgia with me. So do what you have to do to break it off with this guy. I don't want to lose you again. I just can't be without you anymore. Go pick him up, then break up."

He stood up, threw some bills on the table and walked out of the restaurant.

I sat there, holding my breath as his final statements seeped deep into my soul and branded themselves onto the pages of my mind. I peered outside and saw Gerrard hop into his rental car. I could hear the car door slam from inside the restaurant, as well as the tires skidding away. Gerrard was asking me to give up a lot for him at this moment. The only risk he'd taken was visiting me in D.C. If I granted his request to pick up and relocate to Georgia, I had no idea what would await me. Would business be as profitable? Would I like Georgia in general? Would things be stable with Gerrard, or would the joyous reunion wear off after a few months?

With Ray, things were all fresh and new. To me, at the time that Ray and I met, he was a brilliant and vibrant shade of masculinity among a canvas of plastered color gray. He was a protector who made me laugh and was a hopeless romantic. On the downside, the bitter truth was he was barely around because of his job. He had warned me beforehand that his career had been a problem in his past relationships, and at the time I told him that I understood the nature of business and could handle it. As we've grown closer, the trips have gotten tougher for me to deal with. Apparently, his frequent absence was becoming somewhat of a strain to bear.

After I had taken in the events surrounding the past fifteen minutes, I lifted myself from the table and aimlessly wandered to my vehicle. I looked at the digital clock on the face of the radio as I sat in the driver's seat – my arms unable to function to start the ignition. Seven after two. I wanted to be honest with Ray and tell him what had been going on, but I didn't want to risk losing him forever because of my past. Just as I debated where I could go to think uninterrupted for the next hour or so, my cell phone rang.

"This is Sula," I answered flatly with a partial sigh in my voice.

"Hey!" Kaye beamed.

"Don't hey me. I needed to talk to you last night, well, this morning and you hung up on me," I blared.

"I'm sorry, girl. But nothing has changed. You know how I was in college. Cranky as hell and craved my beauty rest."

"Whatever, Kaye. Good thing I wasn't stranded somewhere."

"Sorry! Where are you? I'm out and about I can meet up with you if you're free."

After I gave Kaye the location, she arrived in twenty minutes. She stepped out of her car, tied up her trench and made her way into the diner.

"Hey girl," she greeted jovially. "I see you got the Beemer washed." She chuckled at her own joke, but when I didn't return her sentiment her happiness faded as she read my eyes, "You okay?"

I answered her with tears as I lowered my head. She gave me a comforting hug for a few seconds and then leaned back to take a look at me.

"Sula? What's wrong?"

*　　*　　*　　*

We were finishing up our third cup of coffee in the restaurant where Gerrard and I had just discussed what to do about our futures. Kaye set her cup down and shook her head. After I explained everything to her like a Catholic would to a priest in a confessional booth, her only response was, "Wow."

"What are you going to do?" she asked.

"I don't know. Seeing Gerrard was a dream come true for me. You know that! But meeting Ray was also a dream come true. I don't know what to decide, let alone do." I picked up my coffee cup and twirled around the liquid inside several times as if it were an 8-ball that would reveal all the answers to any question I may have had at that moment. "I have to pick Ray up from the airport soon. Before he left, he said he had something important to discuss with me, but didn't elaborate." I sighed and finalized it with a grunt.

"And you want to tell Ray what's going on?"

"I think it's only fair."

Kaye turned away with smirked lips and raised eyebrows. She took her index finger and lightly scratched the back of her neck.

"What?" I inquired.

"I wouldn't."

I joshed her and she teeter tottered in her seat. I was anxious to hear her reasoning behind this pretentious move in this love game. To me, instances like this had a way of backfiring when you least expected.

"Enjoy yourself," she summed up in two words. "I say screw Gerrard's brains out, then make a decision. If you stay here, you can always visit him in Georgia. Shit girl, have fun."

"I can't do that!" I thought about what I said after the words were released from my mouth. "I mean, not that I can't have fun, but I can't see them both. That's wrong! I wouldn't want either of them to do that to me."

"Sula, you remember earlier this year you told me that you admired me for speaking my mind and doing whatever the hell I wanted?"

I nodded.

"Stop admiring and do it! Neither one of those men are your husband. You think too much." She signaled for the waiter to bring us the check and smoothed out her hair that was packed tightly into a bun.

I looked back into the valley of my coffee cup. The cream and coffee begin to separate, symbolic of my situation with my men, I'd supposed. Do I mix it together and finish it? Or leave it alone?

"But he's talking about me moving to Georgia!"

"Well that's not happening. At least not right away anyway. So you have time."

*   *   *   *

I had parked illegally in the no loading zone at the airport. I saw Ray as he spotted my vehicle and began making his way over to me. His eyes were shaded, but his wide smile that made my heart melt every time, was not. When I saw him striding widely toward me in my rearview mirror with his leather jacket openly exposing his cotton covered pectorals, my body tingled. I shook my head slowly from side to side as I fantasized sexually tearing him apart once we reached our destination.

Without leaving my seat, I popped the trunk. The car bounced as he loaded his two bags inside and slammed it shut. He opened the passenger side door and hopped inside. Before I could say, "hello," he palmed my cheek and planted a butterscotch flavored tongue kiss on me.

"Mmm yummy," I said as I licked my lips and smiled.

"Does this car move?" He asked as he looked at me over the rims of his shades, exposing those big brown eyes.

"Sure does," I said and pulled away into traffic.

On the drive to his house, he told me all about his visits to the various colleges on the west coast, how his meetings went, his night out on the town with all of the prospects – he went on and on about his venture. When it became my turn to recall this weekend's events, it was nowhere near as detailed as his. I summed it up in three activities, working, hanging with friends, and going out to dinner. This clearly wasn't the time to bring up my reunion with my ex-love from college, that's if I was going to bring it up at all.

What concerned me most was what he needed to discuss with me. Instead of me blurting out the question that burned in my throat ready to explode like Mount St. Helens, I relaxed my nerves. He'll talk about it when he's ready. That, however, didn't excuse my anxiousness. Maybe he'd met up with an old friend himself, and was in the same dilemma as I was. That would be cruel poetic justice.

I pulled into the driveway and depressed the button for the trunk release on the way. Once I had parked the car, he hopped out and grabbed his luggage. I met him on the staircase and he handed me his keys to open the front door. I flicked on the switch for the lamp in the dark living room and looked around as if it were the first time I'd seen his home. He had such good taste for a bachelor. As I took in the surroundings and earth tones, I could hear him drop his bags and close the front door behind him. I turned around and he was directly in front of me. I gasped and released a nervous chuckle because I thought he was still by the doorway. He pulled toward him and kissed me deeply. With our lips still pressed together, I could feel him wiggling out of his jacket. I wrapped my arms around his lean back and caressed the entire span of it with my fingertips. I gripped both sides of his waist and slid one hand to his belt buckle. He pulled his lips from mine and looked into my eyes. He looked down at my hand that held on firmly to his belt and waistband on the front of his jeans. Without lifting his head, he scrolled his eyes up slowly and seductively past my frame to meet mine. I lifted one side of my mouth in a smile. He scooped me up in one motion and carried me off into the kitchen, where we ended up making love on the counter, the table, against the fridge and on the floor.

After my slow descent from cloud nine, Ray lifted his masculine naked frame from our position on the floor and went to the bathroom. Moments later, I heard running water. As I lay there with my eyes closed, I imagined we had just made love in a tropical forest next to a fast running stream and he had gone off to find us some fresh fruit to eat. When he returned from the bathroom, I heard him, as his steps grew closer. He kneeled down near my feet and began caressing my legs and hips. I opened my eyes and gently admired the chocolate mass that crouched at the base of my body. The vision alone made my body ready for him yet again. He carefully took my hands and lifted my upper body to an upright position. I folded my legs under me, to balance myself as I moved in to kiss his lips.

"I'm running a hot bath for us," he said in one of the sexiest voices I'd heard him muster.

"Okay, sweetheart."

He helped me to my feet and led me into the bathroom, kissing my shoulders and neck along the way.

We entered the steamy bathroom and shared another kiss before letting the water in the sunken tub envelop us. I dangled my foot over the tub with caution. The vanilla smell from the candles surrounding the tub filled my nostrils as I slowly submerged my foot and let out a low whistle. I slowly brought in my other foot and stood in place to let my nerves get adjusted to the sensation. He stood outside the tub, smiling and wondering if he should step inside.

"How's the water?" he asked.

"Oh, uh, the water's just . . . just fine." I slowly crouched down not looking forward to having my private parts scalded by the near boiling water. As I slowly allowed the water to kiss my bottom, I sucked in the steamy air through my teeth. Ray giggled to himself and decided that it couldn't be that bad.

"I'm just gonna hop in."

And he did.

He wailed for a moment and tried to remain still in order to let his body become acclimated to the heat. Once we both simmered down, I rested my back against his chest and felt his heartbeat. I imitated his breathing pattern and it felt as though we were one person.

"Sula . . ."

"Hmm?" I answered, eyes closed and mind dizzy from the aroma of vanilla steam.

"There's something I want to talk to you about."

I opened my eyes wide, but remained motionless. I swallowed hard and caressed his ankles that rested on the floor of the tub by my hips under the water.

"Sure baby," I said, sounding as sweet and calm as possible, "what's on your mind?" I had no idea what he was about to say as my eyes looked around in a frenzy.

"I'm getting an assistant."

That was it? I thought. He could've saved me a lot of anxiety had he told me this tidbit of information over the phone earlier today. I'll have to see where this conversation is going.

"Okay . . ." I said to give him his cue to continue.

"That's *good* news baby!" he beamed.

"Okay . . ." I said again in the same tone I used earlier. The steam in the bathroom must have been shriveling my brain cells, because I just wasn't following.

"Sula?!" he said in a way that indicated that I should be leaping for joy and smothering his face with kisses. I still wasn't following, so I playfully imitated him.

"Ray?!"

He chuckled. "Baby, I'm going to be sending my assistant to all of these cities and colleges to check out the athletes. He'll be doing the leg work while I set up all of the contacts."

I sat up from his comfortable chest and turned to look into his eyes. He read mine to gather my reaction. A smile slowly crossed my lips, as I understood the magnitude and significance of his "assistant."

"Baby!!!!" I yelped. "That means that . . ."

"Yeah sweetie!"

I turned my body around and straddled his hips as we kissed and rocked back and forth in each other's arms. I placed my palms flat on the wall behind his head and lifted myself up with his help. He placed his hands firmly on my rear, raising my hips onto him. The sweat from our bodies was intertwined with the steamy bath water as we embraced and felt each other's heartbeat.

"Sula?" he summoned, through muffled kisses against my flesh.

"Yes, Ray?" I answered through shortened breaths.

"Stay with me," he commanded as he squeezed my body closer to his.

As we remained in the tub for a few moments more enjoying the warmth and love of each other, I replayed the activities of this weekend in my mind. I had no more questions and no more inner battles. My heart clearly belonged with Ray. He had made a huge sacrifice and did so for us to be together.

I was so elated with his gesture and the fact that he was back in town for good that I quietly wept. The warmth from my tears ran down his chest. He had no idea of my actions. I wanted to selfishly enjoy the revelation that I had just experienced. Ray wasn't asking me to give up my life for him. Instead he was giving up his life for me. In that instant, I was convinced that my searching was over.

Chapter Seventeen - You Can Go Now

"Congratulations, Sula!"

Mr. Toro, the man who owned the coffee shop next door to my gallery, had stopped by briefly to say goodbye. He had a brown paper bag with his shop's logo, which was a caricature of him printed on it. He handed me the bag, which I carefully accepted. I was dumbfounded by his thick New York accented comment. I opened the bag and looked inside to find a half dozen cinnamon and raisin bagels. His bagels weren't the kind that were the size of a standard Hostess donut; they were the size of a towel ring – always fresh, not too chewy. Mr. Toro knew that cinnamon and raisin was my favorite. Over the years he had developed a slight hump in his back. I probably towered over the sweet man about five inches. Don't get me wrong, he didn't look as though he should be ringing some bell in a tower, but his slight deformity probably developed from hand making all of his pastries. That's probably why they were so darn good.

"Congratulations?" I asked, "For what?"

"On the purchase of my property! I was hoping that you would!" He pointed to the bag of bagels. "I hope you enjoy them. I know they're your favorite." He smiled as if he had just found a satchel with wads of cash hidden in his store walls.

"Mr. Toro, I'm afraid I have no idea what you're talking about."

His smile went away for about half a second, and then he replaced it with a smile even wider than the first.

"Oh, Sula, you're so modest. It's a great investment. Keep it as a coffee shop. Fill it with nothing but art books. No music, no newspapers, no television monitors, just art!" He took small steps further into my office with his hand extended for me to accept. "Let's take a look around, shall we?"

"Well . . ." I began to object.

"It'll just take a second."

I took his hand and walked out of the office. I looked at my stack of paper work and pages of thumbnails of art apologetically, as if I could hear them begging me not to leave them.

When we stepped outside, I saw the "sold" sign displayed in his window. I had always entertained the idea of owning his store, but had not had an opportunity to follow up with the investment process when Gerrard came into town last week.

He placed both hands to the glass as he leaned forward to look inside through the binocular-like arc his hands had created.

"Isn't it lovely?"

I leaned closer and peered inside. Instead of seeing all of the loose wires, plaster ridden floors, empty shelves and dust rings from the removed counters, I saw walls of art. Not only that, I saw a few quaint cracked stone top tables that supported art magazines and cups of Frappacino. I envisioned patrons enlisting the help of the employees to discuss the types of art pieces that could be added to their repertoire. And the room was painted in a majestic golden color – with soft orange and rust accents. But when I stepped away from the glass, I saw the dingy gray look of an abandoned shop that was once full of life.

"Mr. Toro," I started, letting go of the dream as I continued to look inside, only to see our reflections in the glass, "I didn't purchase your shop."

"Of course you did."

"Mr. Toro," I repeated, more clearly and firmly, "I didn't buy your shop. I would have loved to but . . ."

"Sula!" a voice called out from the parking lot.

I turned, gave Mr. Toro's hand that dragged me out of my office, a comfortable pat, and spotted Gerrard. He was in an ash gray double-breasted suit, and looked good enough to have a spotlight shone on him.

"Gerrard? I thought you left town?"

"I did. Mr. Toro!" He beamed, shaking his hand, causing the fleshy part of Toro's arm to jiggle. "Gerrard Stiles. Nice to meet you."

Mr. Toro, being the New Yorker that he was, looked at Gerrard up and down as if he had just landed a space shuttle in front of his now vacant establishment.

"Mr. Toro," I helped him to understand, "this is a dear friend of mine from some years back. Gerrard Stiles."

Mr. Toro began to smile again, as he placed his other hand over Gerrard's. "Oh, Gerrard!" he said as if he knew him all the time, but just didn't recognize him, "nice to meet you."

"Yes sir. I purchased your property just yesterday and I'm handing the papers over to Ms. Tyler here."

I looked at him with sheer astonishment plastered over my face. "Gerrard, tell me you didn't do that."

"Mr. Toro," he ignored, "it was nice meeting you. I need to discuss the particulars with Ms. Tyler. We'll see you at the grand opening!"

Gerrard carted me back to the gallery, leaving Mr. Toro standing there like a statue, as he led the way to my office.

When we made it back to my office, Gerrard carefully closed the door behind him, turned to face me and then kissed me.

"Don't thank me."

"Gerrard, what are you doing?" I pushed myself away slightly.

"I'm about to make love to you, Sula baby," he said as he started to unbutton my blouse, but I totally backed myself away from his advances.

"No! Gerrard, why did you do that? Are you trying to buy me?"

He scoffed, "No Sula. It's a gift. No strings attached."

"I don't believe that."

"You don't want it? You know, if you don't want it, I could always set up an office there. We'd be working side by side."

I plopped down in the chair behind my desk and placed my head in my hand. I thought I explained to him that I was in a relationship that was serious. I could've sworn that I told him that it was nice seeing him again to start a new friendship, but my heart belonged to someone else. Now he stood here in my office as if the conversations had never taken place.

"Gerrard, I can't be bought. I'm with someone that I'm very happy with. I'm glad that we got a chance to see each other again, but a friendship is as far as it's going to go."

He reached into his inside suit pocket and pulled out some folded documents. He set them on my desk and caressed them one last time as if he were transferring his pain onto them.

"Sula, it *is* a gift. Just be sure to invite me to the grand opening, okay?" He placed two fingers to his lips, blew me a kiss and then walked away. This time I refused to let him leave. I started out after him, but doubled back to grab the papers. When I made it outside, he was in the middle of the lot.

"Gerrard!" I yelled out.

He turned and stood in place to hear what I had to say. I knew he didn't think I was about to yell my business all over the shopping center, so I lightly jogged over to him.

"Gerrard," I reached for his hand and placed the papers inside it, "I can't accept this."

He nodded and looked at the documents.

"What on earth would Ray say about this? He'd want to know how I managed to make the purchase. Then what would I say? I'm not going to deceive him."

"Sula, please? As a favor to me, please. Just take it." He held out the papers for me. I shook my head and took a step backward. He took my hand and pulled me toward him, and then wrapped his arm around me. He caressed my cheek and pressed a hard closed mouth kiss against my lips. He stuffed the papers into my hand and walked away.

"Gerrard!" I called to him, but this time he continued walking. "Gerrard!"

"I'm glad I found you Sula," he yelled back without turning. He got into his car and drove off, leaving me standing in the parking lot. I looked down at the papers, shook my head and slowly sauntered back into the gallery. I plopped down in my chair and stared at the small bundle of papers as if it was a ticking bomb and I was tasked to disarm it.

I had toiled over the likelihood of never seeing Gerrard again. I didn't want to terminate our association, he was my first love. He said that he would keep in touch and would come back to visit me often, but if my relationship with Ray continued to flourish, I didn't see how that would work - at least not without raising suspicion and a million questions from Ray. I just didn't have the energy for charades with Ray. I'm sure Gerrard and I would still speak on the phone, but I think visiting would not be wise.

Why did he have to buy the place next door? I continued to ask myself over and over again. This was certain to keep us connected, no matter how I looked at the situation. I could only hope that Gerrard would find what he was searching for. After finally seeing Gerrard again and having the opportunity to catch up with him, I felt as though I could close a chapter in my life that has been awaiting finalization after several years.

Chapter Eighteen - The Truth about Chocolate

I got together for happy hour with the girls and was in for some interesting news. It seems that Chocolate Mocha Munch, also known as Harvey, had moved in with Vanessa.

"So what is it, 'Nessa? You drag us all the way out here to Anne Arundel, it'd better be good," Kaye sighed as she twirled the olive around in her martini. "You know gas is high these days."

"It's good, trust me," Vanessa started.

"Okay, spill," Pam ordered as she gulped down the last of her Zombie and gestured for the waiter.

Vanessa smiled wide and tried to cover it with two fingers. "Last night Harvey asked me to marry him." Kaye and I screamed while Pam set her glass down and shook her head in disbelief.

"Where's the ring?" Kaye said, holding her hand out to accept it. I nudged her in the side with my elbow as she chuckled.

"Girl, that's great!" I chimed.

"We're going ring shopping next weekend. We haven't decided on a date yet. Can you believe it? I'm so excited!" She hopped up and down in her seat, spilling her drink over the tabletop. Kaye quickly grabbed a linen napkin to sop up the liquid before it crept its way from the table to her skirt.

"Girl, will you watch what your excited ass is doing?" Kaye scorned while wiping up the mess and giving a light chuckle.

"What in the world made him ask?" Pam asked flatly with her lips pursed.

"Uhh, *me!*" Vanessa said loudly, "I'm a damn good woman."

"You're not all that!" I playfully interjected. "No, for real, you enjoy being tossed around in the air by that fine chocolate man! Wooo!"

All of us laughed except for Pam. Instead she leaned back in her chair and slouched. Her eyes looked glazed over as the waiter set down another Zombie in front of her. I gave Pam a scornful expression when I noticed her gestures, while she just shrugged and rolled her eyes to the ceiling.

Kaye leaned over to me and whispered in my ear, "that's *your* friend."

"What's going on Pam? I know we all ordered drinks based on our mood, but what's up with the

Zombie?" I asked while sipping my 'Sex with an Alligator'.

"I feel like a Zombie, that's why," she spat out rudely.

There was a brief silence for a moment, as Kaye stared at me, shook her head and sipped her Vodka martini. Vanessa sighed and swirled the liquid in her glass with a straw. Pam on the other hand, swallowed down half of her drink in one gulp and was really getting on my nerves with her attitude.

"Pam," I started, "what's wrong with you? Why you acting like an ass?"

"Tell me about it," Kaye signified under her breath.

"You know what, I don't want to be an ass, so I'll just leave," she stood up grabbed her drink, swallowed the rest down and started out. I stood up to stop her.

"Pam, sober up first. Relax," I guided her back to the table and sat her down. Kaye threw her eyes up to the ceiling and shifted in her seat restlessly. Vanessa watched the whole exchange, her face void of expression. "What's on your mind, girl?"

"You wanna know?"

"I asked."

"I don't," Kaye said coolly.

"You *really* wanna know? Fine, I'll tell you. Vanessa, do you have any idea what you are about to marry?"

"Oh brother . . ." I started. I thought to myself, *why did I even bother to ask what was on her deluded, drunken mind?*

"I know he dances and all that. I don't care," Vanessa defended her Chocolate Mocha Munch.

"All that?" Pam scoffed, "you sure you know what *all that* is?"

"Pam? Did you hear me? I do not care. He's with me *now*," Vanessa's neck slightly jerked with each syllable. I could tell Pam was about to push Vanessa to her brink. After all of the nonsense with Kenard, I supposed Vanessa was well equipped to push back.

"*Right now* is more like it," she gestured for the waiter to bring her another drink by holding up her empty glass high in the air. Vanessa pushed away from the table and prepared to stand. Kaye placed a calming hand on her shoulder that kept her in the seat.

I looked over to Kaye and jerked my head quickly to the right to beckon her to get Vanessa away from Pam before we were all on the news that evening. Kaye picked up on the hint just after my fifth head movement and carted Vanessa off with her uttering obscenities along the way.

"Girl, what is wrong with you?" I scooted my chair closer to Pam.

"She has no idea of who Chocolate Mocha Munch aka Harvey is."

"Yes she does. You don't think that they've talked about his past while planning for their future? Or maybe she doesn't *want* to concentrate on his past. Did you think about that?"

"Sula, spare me please," she calmly stated as the waiter plopped down another drink in front of her. I quickly grabbed it and placed it on the opposite side of the table out of her reach.

"Are you jealous of Vanessa because she's getting married?"

Pam scoffed and then let out a hard chuckle, "Please, okay? I don't even now Vanessa."

"Then, what's the problem?"

"Sula, Chocolate danced at a party one of my girlfriends threw a couple of weeks ago." She reached over the table clumsily and grabbed the glass, spilling liquid onto the tabletop.

"So?"

"He was with three girls who paid him $300 each. He's a ho, okay? How you gonna change *that* into a husband? A faithful one at that?" her words slurred.

I sighed heavily and searched for words to answer her question. I didn't want to get involved in Vanessa and Harvey's relationship, but I'm sure Vanessa was going to want some sort of explanation regarding Pam's odd behavior this evening. As I blankly stared at Pam slurping down her Zombie, I had no idea what to do. I wasn't sure if I should tell Vanessa or just stay the hell out of it.

"And to top it all off, I got a visit from my ex-husband the other week. He just felt the need to tell me that he reconnected with his first love. We filed for divorce and it hadn't even been a year! I tried to be his everything, but I couldn't measure up with an old fantasy. He screwed my life up. So this Zombie is for him! Rot in hell, Gerrard."

I nearly fainted from what I heard. It couldn't be my Gerrard. It just wasn't possible.

"What was his last name?" I asked after I calmed my heartbeat.

She huffed, "Stiles. It's funny how people have names that describe the opposite of what they are or possess. Like Grace and, and Faith and eh, Stiles."

I stared at her intently. I had no words and certainly did not want to tell the girls about this. At least not right now. I just wanted to leave.

*   *   *   *

When I came back from my get together, Ray was lounging on my couch snoring so loud; I thought there was a bear growling in the room. He sat up a little and moaned as my footstep creaked on the floor disturbing his slumber.

"Sula? You back?" he grumbled softly.

I knelt beside him and caressed his forehead down to his cheek. I kissed his lips softly.

"Yes, baby. Come to bed," I instructed as I reached for his hand. He cracked his eyes a little and managed to focus in on my smiling face. He grinned at me and then chuckled softly. "What?" I curiously asked.

"There's a drink umbrella in your hair."

I awkwardly tried to look up as if I would be able to see the top of my head. I reached up and roughly patted my head a few times to locate the exact spot where the umbrella was hidden. I felt the toothpick and paper creation, pulled it out and inspected it. "Kaye," I said out loud with a scoff.

Ray sat up in the chair and tasted the insides of his mouth as he looked around the room through squinted eyes. I relaxed myself and sat further down on the floor, giving my knees a rest. I looked into my lap, shook my head and then looked up at Ray.

"What's the matter?" he asked with a scruffy voice. He yawned immediately after and reached out his hand for me to join him on the couch.

"Vanessa's about to marry a ho and doesn't know it. Pam told me something about Vanessa's soon to be husband and then dropped a fucking H-Bomb on me about her ex."

"Whoa, and you dropped the f-bomb. And Vanessa's marrying a ho?" he asked as he raised his head in shock. He rested back down when I nodded, and then said, "Does she know? Marriage is an important step."

"I don't know, and people don't accept the truth well. Or they think any bad news or negative opinions means you're jealous."

"Which loosely translated means they are having doubts themselves. Well, how do you think she would feel if she found out that you knew something about her man and didn't bother to tell her? She'd never speak to you again. So, let's say you tell her, she discards it, it comes back to bite her, she's the one that has to eat crow and give the old *you were right, I was wrong* spiel," he shifted a bit to get more comfortable and then said "Just think about it. And what's the deal with Pam's ex?"

"Oh! Nothing," I responded flatly. "This world is too damn small. Sorry for cursing earlier."

*   *   *   *

The next day I met up with Vanessa and decided that no matter how our conversation went, I was not going to tell her that Pam used to be married to Gerrard. She did not need to know and I was still processing it myself.

"Since I'm getting married, do you think Ray will propose anytime soon?" Vanessa asked as she flipped through a bridal magazine.

"Girl, please. You know how I get if I get the slightest inkling. I totally run with it. Lessoned learned, so I'm just enjoying it. I don't want to think that far ahead," I responded while looking out of the subway window of the Metro at the graffiti painted walls of stone.

"Well, maybe he and Harvey should hang out. Harvey has his mind on marriage. Maybe it will rub off on Ray."

"Ray hang out with Harvey? Not happening."

"You know, contrary to what you guys saw at the strip club, Harvey is a real sweetie. We talk all the time. That is the most important thing, Sula. If you can't communicate with your man, forget it. When you grow old with that person, they may not be able to do the physical things that they're used too, but if they can speak, they'll always have great conversation. At 80 years old, sometimes that's the most important thing."

"Does he tell you about his work?" I pried innocently.

"Sometimes. I mean, he told me about some gig he had a few weeks ago."

I tilted my head and looked deeply in Vanessa's eyes. I wondered if this was the same gig that Pam mentioned. Then I wondered if Chocolate told her exactly what went down at that gig and the whole story regarding it.

"And?" I asked.

"And he got paid very well that night. Almost twelve hundred dollars."

"Just for dancing?"

"I doubt it. I mean, I know he's fine, but come on, would y'all pay $1200 for him to take his clothes off?"

"What the hell are you saying, Vanessa?"

"I don't wanna know what he does or how he gets his money right now. He's doing this for us. He comes home every night and I know he loves me."

She looked down in her magazine and flipped through a few more pages. She sighed slowly and pressed her lips together.

"Do you know what he did?"

I shook my head.

"He handed me all of the money. We're saving for our wedding and a down payment on a new house. Screw these desperate ho's out here, Sula. That man is mine."

Chapter Nineteen - That Dream was Real!

I was designing the tabletop and floor display for my booth at the Sisters of D.C. Convention when I heard the front door to the gallery open. I was going to display some of the top prints my gallery sold and debut my artwork for the first time. I heard a few giggles exchanged between Gayle and Tara before I heard the bass from a male voice. I tilted my head closer to the entrance of my office to hear a little better, but it didn't help. I couldn't make out a single word from the deep mumbles. I shrugged it off and continued to design the backdrop for the booth. There was a light tapping on the door when I looked up and noticed Tara.

"Sula? You have a visitor," she notified me with a wide grin.

I looked at her suspiciously and narrowed my eyes, "Who?"

"It's me, Sula," Gerrard said as he appeared from behind Tara, "again."

I smiled slightly as I stared up at him. I was a bit annoyed with the unannounced visits and flashed a quick glare to Tara as if she had committed some heinous crime.

"I'll leave you two to talk," she whispered as she backed out of the office and closed the door quietly.

"Gerrard . . ."

"Before you get started . . .," he reached in his breast pocket and pulled out a folded envelope. "Here." He placed the envelope on my desk and sat down. Knowing what the contents already were, I picked it up, sat across from him and crossed my legs.

"You drove all the way from Atlanta to return this?" I said as I inspected my handwriting on the letter.

"First of all, I didn't drive, I flew. Secondly, yes. I came back here to give you that. I was offended when it showed up in my mailbox," he shook a scolding finger at me and proceeded to unbutton his suit jacket. He pulled his ankle over the knee of his opposite leg and leaned back in the chair. "Plus, I just wanted to see you again."

"Gerrard, I don't want this back. And the mild stalking has to stop," I said extending the letter for him to take it.

"Stalking? Come on. Well, if you don't want it, tear your check up. I don't want your money. You know what I want," he smiled slyly and looked at my cleavage.

I looked down at my bosom, then up at Gerrard. I gave him a reprimanding look and leaned all the way back in the chair to deter his roving eyes.

"Gerrard, I know it's not the entire amount, but five thousand isn't a skimpy first installment. I appreciate you getting the property next door for me, but I intend to pay you for it. I told you that. No strings."

"It was a gift. I mean it, Sula. Don't send me anymore money," he clasped his hands together and gulped hard as if he was preventing himself from choking on his words. "I won't accept it."

My eyes focused on his and saw the seriousness they expressed. I took a huge breath and tore up the letter and tossed it into the wastebasket. "Fine," I surrendered. "You could've told me that over the phone, you know."

"Like I said, I wanted to see you again anyway," he paused and scoffed before he spoke, "Would you have torn up the check over the phone?"

"No, I would've carted it right back to the mailbox."

"I'm prepared to do what it takes to get you back," he told me. "I will win you back."

I was in no mood for Gerrard and his mind games. As he sat across from me, I imagined him with Pam. To me, she was the woman who stole my proposal. It was silly for me to be upset, but it bothered me. Perhaps because I knew of Pam's past. It was a bit ironic how she was ready to destroy Vanessa and Chocolate's plans for marriage, when her lifestyle at one time mirrored Chocolate's. What a hypocrite. There was no need to discuss this with Gerrard. He had no idea that Pam and I knew each other. Besides, I didn't want to give him the satisfaction. We are over.

My intercom buzzed and Tara's voice emanated the office through the speaker phone. Gerrard and I listened intently to what she was about to say.

"Sula? Can you pick up please?"

I grabbed the phone from the cradle and placed it to my ear. Gerrard cleared his throat and awkwardly looked me in the face to see if my expressions would offer any indication of what issue disturbed our brief meeting.

"No, it's okay," I said and then hung up.

"Client?"

"Uh, no. Actually that was uh . . ." I started. Then the door opened slowly. Ray poked his head in and smiled at me. When he saw Gerrard, his smile dissolved.

"Oh! I didn't know you were meeting with a client. I can wait," Ray offered. Gerrard looked at me partially surprised. It was time for Gerrard to see who that someone else was in my life. He would be leaving here knowing that he could not just hop a plane and come to D.C. whenever he got good and ready.

"Are you her boyfriend? Ray, right?" Gerrard stood and extended his hand for Ray to shake.

"Yeah," he replied cautiously gripping Gerrard's hand firmly. I took a moment to take a sip of water from my water bottle. My mind played out a terrible scene of them slugging it out right there in the office and destroying my exhibit for the conference. Ray was probably wondering how this person knew him without knowing in turn who he was. The lukewarm water was swallowed with a hard gulp before I took a deep breath. I set the bottle down without recapping it.

"I'm Gerrard Stiles."

Ray squinted and tilted his head slightly with a grin. He shook his hand slower and slower until he could make a connection.

"Sula and I went to the same college," Gerrard sat down and looked at me with a devilish grin. I supposed he had suddenly realized that I hadn't mentioned a peep of my reunion with him or who he was exactly for that matter. I was petrified by what Gerrard may say next.

"Oh okay," Ray took a seat in a vacant chair and kept his eyes on Gerrard. I brandished a dumb smile and breathed in and out more quickly. I took another sip of the warm water.

"Yeah, we went to undergrad together."

"Oh okay. So Gerrard, what brings you by?" Ray inquired.

"I was just talking to Ms. Tyler here about investing in her business. She's expanding to the vacant spot next door."

"Babe, you didn't tell me that. That's great!" Ray answered. Gerrard grinned at me, but I felt as though he was guffawing loudly on the inside at Ray's ignorance.

"It was supposed to be a surprise, honey," I lied.

"Well, then Gerrard you should invest," Ray suggested to him. "My lady's making some positive moves in her career. It's best to get on the investment bus while there are empty seats, man."

Gerrard stood to his feet as he laughed and nodded at Ray's inside business tip. "You're right. Hey, I'm about to get on outta here. I know Sula has a lot to do. Hey! You want to join me for a quick drink, Ray? Sula can catch up with us when she's done here."

My eyes widened as I stared at Gerrard, totally speechless. Ray looked at me and pointed innocently to Gerrard before he spoke.

"Sure, why not? You mind sweetie? Come join us when you're done. It'd be nice to hear about your college high jinks," he winked and laughed loudly as he patted Gerrard on the back as they headed out.

I stood up to stop them from leaving, but ending up spilling my water all over the desk instead.

"Shit!" I mumbled. By the time I grabbed up the half empty bottle and scrambled to find napkins to sop up the mess before the art magazine did, those guys were gone. "Great. That's perfect!" I yelled out to no one in particular.

I flopped down in my chair and looked at the clock that read four thirty. My mind wandered as I focused on the clock absent-mindedly. I snapped out of my trance and tried my best to finish arranging the display. I knew I wouldn't be able to finish it now because my mind kept wondering what those two men would be discussing. For the moment, the best I could do was jot down the way I wanted the items displayed. I was ready to get on the road to meet up with them. A past and present mate's banter over liquor didn't set well with me. Before I knew it, it was almost five thirty when my phone rang.

"Sula Tyler," I answered.

"Hey sweetheart, we're at Mango Mike's. You coming?" The Reggaeton music blared over Ray's slurred words.

"Are you okay?" I shouted so he could hear me.

"Just come on down, okay?"

"Is Gerrard still with you?"

"I'll see you in a bit," he uttered and then hung up.

"Hello? Hello?" I asked of the dial tone on the other end of the receiver. My heart sank low in my chest just before it began doing round-offs. I shut down my computer and neatened up the stacks of work on my desk that had gone unattended since this afternoon. I grabbed my purse, darted out of the office and locked the doors behind me – I think.

As I had suspected, traffic was heavier than usual downtown and I knew it would only get worse the closer I got to my destination. I heard several songs play on the radio as I waited for my turn to go at several stoplights. After hearing Cee-lo Green's "Like a Fool" for the third time in only forty minutes, I pounded the 'off' button on the radio and huffed loudly. I pressed the horn on my car long and hard, which triggered a chain reaction of other horns blaring off behind me.

"Come on, people!" I yelled behind raised car windows. Straightening my back, I sat up in my seat and peered over the hood to see what the holdup was. There were three people arguing in the middle of the street over what appeared to be a slight fender bender.

"Can't they take that to the side?" I asked myself out loud. I waited for about ten more seconds and

wheeled my car wildly into the right lane. My foot
mashed the gas pedal to the floor as my car screeched
away from the scene as I barreled to yet another red light.
I growled under my breath and rested my head back on
the headrest. I checked my wristwatch and sighed again.

When I finally arrived at Mango Mike's, I got lucky
and found a spot not far from the entrance. The place was
packed! I smiled and raised my clasped hands to the
heavens and quickly parked into the available spot. I
raced out of my car and dashed inside the restaurant.

The hostess tried to stop me, but I brushed past her
to find Ray. I spotted him and Gerrard in the back
downing shots of brown liquid and laughing. I smiled
awkwardly at the two and waited for one of them to offer
me a seat as I wondered just how trashed they were.

Ray smiled when he saw me and stood up. He
greeted me with a quick peck and gave me his seat.

"Here's my girl," Ray giggled as he eyed me
seductively.

"You guys been drinking the whole time you've
been here?" I chuckled lightly as I slowly slid into the
seat.

"We had a few before happy hour started," Ray
confessed. "You want something to eat, sweetie?"

"Um . . ." I started, but Gerrard interrupted me.

"Do you still make that killer beef stroganoff of
yours, Sula?" he asked, as he leaned over the table to put
his face in mine and gave me a knowing smile. "I *still*
haven't had beef stroganoff as good as yours." He gulped
down his chaser and rested his cheek on his palm, staring

at me with dreamy eyes. "It was so tasty. The best I've ever had."

Gerrard winked at me and raised his eyebrows. Ray shot him a perturbed look as I began to break out in a sweat. I knew what the hell he meant.

"It's a simple recipe," I said trying to play it off by pretending he was talking about the actual dish. I looked over the menu quickly and told Ray to order me the red beans and rice, which I never ate. "'Cuse me, guys," I said as I grabbed my purse and started to bolt toward the restroom, almost toppling over a waiter.

"No problem baby," Gerrard said. "Be mine and I'll be thine! Right?" He winked at me and chuckled. Ray shot Gerrard a damning look then peered furiously at me. I gave a nervous chuckle and quickly left to avoid an intense line of questioning and subsequent argument.

When I got into the restroom, I stared at myself in the mirror for a while before grabbing my loose hair and pulling it into a tight ponytail with my hands. After I could feel some strands being pulled from the root, I let go and threw my head back and stared at the ceiling. A woman entered, dressed in a stunning navy blue suit.

"You alright, girl?" she inquired.

"What is it about ex's not wanting you to be with anyone else, huh?" I asked the ceiling, but directed the question to her.

"Are you talkin' about them two fine men out there?"

I looked at her this time, "Um, yeah."

"You seeing both of 'em or something?" She grabbed a tissue and blotted her makeup.

"One I used to see a long time ago."

"I don't mean no harm, but if it was me, I'd *still* be seeing both of 'em. Girl, they are fine!" She reached in her purse as she laughed and pulled out a tube of lipstick.

"You sound like one of my girlfriends," I sighed and tried to smile.

"That's a wise woman," she patted me on the shoulder. "Don't mind me, honey. I just got out of a relationship and turned every other brother down because I was trying to be faithful. Now that he's gone, I wish I would've at least tested those waters. But, you do *your* thang," she smiled and walked out.

I stared at myself a little while longer and decided to change my attitude from solemn to charming before I headed back to the men. Something in the pit of my stomach told me that I shouldn't have let Ray come to happy hour with Gerrard. Since we were here, I just had to make the best of it and end the night as quickly as possible before a cross-examination transpired.

When I arrived at the table, Ray was standing by it while he watched me approach him. I smiled and placed my hand on the chair to seat myself. He gripped my arm and gave me a slight tug. I looked up in his eyes surprised by the gesture. I glanced over at Gerrard who avoided eye contact with me as he continued to nurse his drink. He flaunted a smirk as he looked in the glass.

"What's wrong, honey?" I asked Ray.

"We're leaving. Let's go."

"Did you order my rice?"

Instead of responding, he carted me out of the restaurant quickly. I tried to look back at Gerrard, but my head couldn't turn that far around. The patrons continued with their conversations, imbibing, joking, and eating as we whisked by them to the exit and out of the front door.

Once we were outside, I stood in front of Ray to get him to stop walking so fast. I nearly tripped on the raised slab of concrete on the sidewalk. I placed my hands on his chest to stop him.

"Ray! What is going on?"

"Get in the car, Sula. We'll talk in there," he stood by the passenger side of my car as I walked around to unlock the door to let us both inside.

He sat down and nearly cracked the glass in the door by the force he used to slam it shut.

"What is wrong?" I nearly yelled this time.

"You *fucked* him?"

I sat in the seat staring at Ray as I tried to resume breathing. My heart pounded in my chest faster than a tribal drum during a ceremonial ritual. I took a deep breath as I tried to figure out what to say to him.

"What?" I could barely believe what he just asked me. I'm sure at some point of the conversation Gerrard let Ray know that we used to date in college, so of course we did it! However, the way the question was posed didn't sound as if he was referring to the past.

"Are you out of your mind, Sula!? Gerrard told me everything, so you'd better start talking!"

"Wait wait…what are you talking about? What did he tell you?"

"Really? Really? That's the game you want to play? Look, when you were in the bathroom, Gerrard's lips got loose. He told me about y'alls relationship in school, the proposal at graduation, all that! He tracked you down and saw you last week. The week I was out of town? What the fuck, Sula? He knew what I had inscribed on the bracelet that I spent my hard earned money on? There's only one way he could've saw it! He bought that store for you? What did you give him for that?" he stared at me, teeth gnashed and awaited an answer.

"What? No!"

"Did he buy the store next door for you or not?" Ray yelled.

"Yes, but Ray, wait a minute! Just listen to me!" I reached for his hands but he pulled away from me. I gasped as the tears welled up in my eyes. I could barely speak.

"I don't need to listen to you! I got my answer. That's just great, Sula!" he said as he stared out of the window while he shook his head at whatever was going on in his mind. Before he opened the car door, Ray stared at me deep in my eyes.

"Ray…" I mustered.

"Don't call me. It's clear that you still have some feelings for this long lost love. Yeah, I remember you telling me about it on the dinner cruise. That's him, huh? I didn't know this guy was gonna pop up one day. And you'd sleep with him. Since this is gonna be an issue, just keep me out of it. You stay away from me."

"I didn't sleep with him! He's not an issue, Ray. He's in the past!"

"That's why the past was in your office when I got there? That's why when you saw him, you slept with your past!?" Ray scoffed.

"No! I didn't!"

Ray took in a large amount of air as he closed his eyes tight and whispered, "Damn, Sula. Damn. Damn. I loved you..."

"Ray, Gerrard is lying! He's not a part of my life anymore!" The thought of Ray leaving me for good made my heart ache from its hard and rapid pounding. "I love you so much, Ray. I need you!"

"He's lying? You saw him behind my back! You're not denying that. He bought the store next door for you, Sula! Don't you understand I don't trust you!?" he said, "Just leave me alone."

"But I didn't do anything!"

Ray got out of the car and slammed the door behind him. He hopped into his car and sped off. I dropped my head and looked in my lap. My hands were shaking and the tears were streaming. This was the fork in the road to our relationship that I knew would appear at some point. I had no inkling when we first met and began our journey that the trial would be over a false accusation regarding fidelity. I just wanted the drama kept at bay. First the Pedro kiss, now an old flame. If the tables were turned I wouldn't trust me either. All I knew was I had to fix it. I didn't want to lose Ray, especially since I made the decision in my heart that he was the person I wanted to be with. Ray took the word of a drunken stranger over the woman he'd been laying with for months who he claimed he loved.

Ray was finished with me.

Chapter Twenty - What now?

Now that the damage was done, the irony of it all was that I hadn't heard a word from Gerrard. No surprise visits, no letters in the mail, no phone calls. It was a classic case of "if I can't have you, no one will." I tried to understand what would make him lie about us having sex. I could explain away the store next door with the check that I wrote him. No wait, I threw that away. Well, at least it was in my ledger, but I supposed that wouldn't have mattered. The issue of sex would be hard to explain. It was Gerrard's word against mine. Or Gerrard using Ray's words from the bracelet against mine. Ray clearly had his mind made up that I was some Jezebel who couldn't be trusted whenever he went out of town. I tried to contact him several times. He had no office, so I couldn't pop up there. I had no idea what else to do. I'd already gone by his house; he refused to even come to the door. I'm not even sure if he got the letter that I left in his door frame. I felt desperate going through such lengths, but I loved him. I was not going to let him leave my life over a lie.

I had an unfinished painting in the corner that I was going to add to the Sister conference. I didn't even feel like finishing it. I just wanted to melt away and stay hidden until the pain subsided. I only wished he'd given me the chance to explain, but he was so upset about the whole situation. He didn't even look at me – he didn't want me to touch him. I was hurting all over. I couldn't talk to Vanessa or Kaye. I feared I would break into tears before even explaining what had happened. I wanted to call Gerrard to curse his ass out, but I didn't want to give him the satisfaction of knowing he destroyed my relationship.

I reflected on the dream of them together. The final motion they both made. Shunning me and not speaking any further. I was so tempted to fly my ass back to Africa and explain to the old woman that she needed to redip this bracelet in more ancestral water or antelope piss, whatever the hell she used, because I was single again.

*   *   *   *

As I drove home from the office, I listened to the weather forecast that called for a severe snowstorm to hit our area in the next few days. I took a detour and decided to go to the grocery store to pick up a few essentials. One thing about D.C., if half an inch of snow was predicted, all the eggs, milk, bread, water – everything, even the shopping carts, would be gone in a flash. Sometimes, I wished the entire area would just get a grip.

I thought about how it would've been if Ray and I were snowed in together. We would've had so much fun. Laughing, cooking . . . well, I would've been cooking, and us making love. At the thought of it, I huffed loudly and walked briskly toward the living room. I flopped down on the couch and started punching numbers in on the keypad of the telephone. I wasn't in the mood to cook either, so I ordered a pizza instead. That would last me for a few days before I started attacking the groceries I had bought.

Once the pizza had arrived, I opened it and took a huge bite out of one slice. That was really all I could stand to eat. I know it had only been a few days, but I had lost at least five pounds. I just didn't want to do anything right now except cry. I ran my fingers through my hair and rested them on the crown of my head. I closed my eyes and recalled that night as if someone had taken a picture and placed it on the counter next to the pizza box for me to see. Just as an onslaught of tears were about to be released, my phone rang.

Please let it be Ray, I thought. When I looked at the caller i.d., my shoulders dropped.

"Hey Vanessa," I flatly said.

"The wedding is off," she said.

"What?! Why?"

"I can't do it, Sula. I just can't," she admitted. "Something is telling me not to do it, so I'm going to trust my instincts for once. He's fine, but looks fade and muscles turn to fat. Not to mention, I don't really agree with how he makes his money. You can't turn a ho into a husband."

Good, I thought to myself. I got so wrapped up in the foolishness with Gerrard and Ray, I didn't even have a chance to tell her what Pam had told me about Harvey. This way I won't ever have to.

"Wow. Well, how are you feeling?" I asked her. I tried to keep myself together to hear her response, and then I would get her off of the phone so I could have my own pity party in peace.

"I'm actually okay. I just wanted to tell you that," she said. "I will let you go, I know that you and Ray are about to get cozy in the love nest."

I almost released an agonizing gut wrenching scream in her ear when she said that.

"Yeah...," I said with a sigh. "I'll holler at you later. Sorry about your friend."

"It's okay," she finalized. "I wanted you to be the first to know."

After I hung up with Vanessa, I decided to do something I told myself I wouldn't. I called Gerrard. He at least owed me some sort of explanation and I certainly needed one. The man who once brought me happiness, who was my heart's main reason for beating, was the same man who tore it to pieces with his slanderous words. He broke my heart not once, but twice now. He clearly wasn't the man for me, but I needed to know. I needed closure yet again.

"Hey Sula!" he answered as if nothing had occurred.

"Gerrard, just tell me why you told him that," I asked.

"Told who what?"

"Cut the shit, Gerrard! You know what I'm talking about!" I yelled in the receiver.

"There's no need to curse at me, baby. I did you a favor, that dude wasn't strong enough for you. Let me guess, he got pissed off and broke up with you?" he nonchalantly summated.

"Ya think?"

"Sula, do you want someone who is going to take the word of someone they don't know over yours? He's not a self thinker. What an easy target," he chuckled. "At least now we can be together with no interferences."

I held the phone and could barely believe what I was hearing. It was true, I loved Gerrard. Loved. Now, I had to permanently close that door and open a new one. I was unsure if Ray would be in my future or not, but I knew that Gerrard would not be. How could he love me like he says if he had no problem stealing my happiness?

"No sweetheart, we can't. I'm sorry, Gerrard," I began, "but it's over between you and I. I hope that you continue to do well. Goodbye."

I hung up the phone, tossed myself onto my bed and cried until I fell asleep.

Chapter Twenty One - Now I'm Found

The storm that the National Weather Service predicted would blanket the D.C. area by 14 inches never came. However, D.C. ended up with two inches of rain instead. In a panic, D.C. had purchased every loaf of bread, jug of water and other non-perishable, once again, making several entrepreneurs filthy rich. I thought it was all a conspiracy, but it was for the sake of the economy, right?

Despite the frigid temperatures, I met up with Kaye and Vanessa for Sunday brunch. As Vanessa prattled on about the cancellation of her wedding plans, my mind tuned her out and focused in on my own personal issues with Ray. I had dissected our relationship and put it back together again several times in my head.

Here I was again, doing the same thing. I had punished myself enough for Lawrence breaking up with me and I certainly didn't want a rerun of emotions with Ray. The break up impacted me and the bottom line was that I was missing Ray. We fit together and I craved his touch, his conversation, his laughter and his love.

"What do you think?" I sort of heard Vanessa ask. "Sula?"

"I agree," I said flatly, staring into my plate of uneaten food.

"Hmm…are you okay?" she asked.

"Yeah, you're not eating," Kaye pointed her fork in the direction of my dish.

"I'm fine, why?" I lied.

"Because Sula, I was talking about this guy at work. All he does is talk on the phone and I busted him having sex with this temp in the supply room. The bum said that I was jealous because I wanted him to do it to me and you say *I agree*?" Vanessa stated as she folded her arms with a pouted mouth.

"I apologize. My mind is somewhere else."

"No shit," Kaye said as she stuffed a chunk of pineapple in her mouth.

"So what's up?"

"I don't understand men at all," I said through a heavy sigh.

Kaye dropped her fork noisily down onto her plate and stared blankly at me before she made her declaration. "Join the club! Look girl, I'm about to give you the best advice you're ever gonna get, so listen close. Stop trying to understand them and enjoy them."

"How can I when they keep playing a bunch of games?" I queried.

"See, you're not listening. I said enjoy *them*. That's plural," Kaye winked at me as she sipped her orange juice.

"Something happened between you and Ray," Vanessa concluded instead of just asking me.

"Well, yeah. He broke up with me. Told me never to call him again," I jabbed at my food with my fork as my eyes welled up.

"You're kidding, right?" Kaye asked.

"Nope."

"You still got Gerrard's number?"

"Kaye?" I mustered through a labored breath, "I want to be with Ray. Gerrard lied on me to Ray. I want Ray."

"Call him and tell him so," Vanessa volunteered.

Unfortunately, what sounded simple to them was not the case at all. Ray would rather be stubborn than in love. No matter how many times I explored the different paths of my relationship with Ray, it all led to the same destination – togetherness. However, togetherness did not appear to be an option. When he told me in the car that he loved me, meaning he no longer did, he said it as if he had made a huge mistake in dealing with me. As if I had manipulated his emotions just to reel him in and drive him away.

*   *   *   *

I went straight home after finishing brunch with the girls to mope in peace. I put in my custom made

Stevie Wonder cd that would become the soundtrack to another private pity party hosted by me. Ironically, the first song on the play list was "All is Fair in Love". Upon the first note, I went to the bathroom to grab the box of Kleenex and the wastebasket, so I wouldn't have to move for the next hour or so.

During that song, I reflected on the good times in our relationship. The bubble baths, the evening cruise, spurs of the moment road trips, the way he danced and how he laughed at my dumb jokes. These reflections of our love only prepared me for an all out bawling session when "Blame It on the Sun" played next. After that song, I had to turn off the music. Although Stevie's voice could make the most melodious angel in heaven jealous, he was making me miserable.

I had given thoughts of Ray a rest for the moment and began reflecting on my life in general. I looked back on past years and realized that everyone in my life served a specific purpose. In retrospect, I don't regret a thing.

No matter how much Lawrence may have hurt me, he taught me how to let go. Although my time with Pedro was brief, he taught me how to appreciate other cultures. Gerrard helped me close an important chapter of my life. Before he showed up in my office, I had always wondered in the back of my mind what had happened to him. Pam, although I don't necessarily agree with her methods, showed me what focus and determination meant to achieve your goals. Whatever the goal may be. Vanessa really tested my ability to be a friend no matter what situations surrounded us. Kaye, with her crazy self, always keeps it real and makes me appreciate the gift of laughter despite any bad circumstance. As for my Ray, he taught me how to love again. Even though he's gone, I now know not to allow anyone to interfere with what is important to me. I shouldn't have given that much latitude to Gerrard, especially when I knew I was in love with Ray. It was over.

Just as I was listening to the crackle of wood in the fireplace and staring at the dance of the flames, the doorbell rang.

I sat there hoping the person would go away. I was in no state of mind to talk to anyone and certainly didn't feel up to directing any strangers to a neighbor's house. The doorbell rang again. I quickly wiped my face and went to answer the determined visitor. I opened the door and stood frozen.

It was Ray and he was covered with snow. He stared at me and didn't say anything, but his eyes pleaded to be let inside. Speechless, I opened the door. As he came in, I looked past him and stared outside with widened eyes. The whole neighborhood was blanketed with snow, and it was falling pretty fast. I closed the door and turned to face him.

He reached for my hand. After I accepted it, he pulled me close to him and hugged me tight. I silently wept as he held on to me for what felt like hours. No words were exchanged, just the warmth from our bodies.

"If I was gonna be snowed in, I wanted to be snowed in with you," he told me and kissed me gently on the forehead. He led me over to the fireplace.

"I missed you so much," I said as I caressed his face.

"If we're going to be doing this for the rest of our lives, we may as well start tonight. I've thought a lot about us while we were apart, baby."

"Ray, nothing happened. I swear to you."

"I should've known you wouldn't hurt me. It's just...,"

"I'm so sorry, Ray."

"I love you, Sula. I know how Gerrard must've felt knowing that you moved on. And I know that he probably would've said or done anything to mess up what you had. It took me a while to um, to realize that. I read your note that you left explaining everything that happened. And I appreciate your candor, and for being vulnerable. I know I must've said some harsh things to you and I'm sorry."

I looked deep into his eyes and gently stroked his hand.

"I just had a lot of time to think over the past few weeks. I don't want to be without you. So I was out a lot, trying to find um...well," he began. He tiptoed around his words as if he wanted to say the right thing. He held my hand, took a deep breath and continued, "I want to say this to you now, so there is no misunderstanding. I want you to be my wife."

I almost fell over but managed to reply, "What? You're proposing?"

"Yes. I want you to be my wife next year," he said. He dropped down on one knee, pulled a jewelry box from his pocket, and took my hand. It remained closed while he spoke.

The last time I thought I was getting a proposal, it went terribly awry. I honestly thought that Ray was joking at first and was going to take it too far. I was just happy he was here with me and accepted my apology. The extra theatrics weren't necessary. He could be a jokester at times. But when he got down to formally propose, I almost lost my breath. My heart pounded so hard I thought it was over working itself and I'd faint. My hands began to shake slightly.

"Sula, you and I have both had a number of hurts in our lives, but I couldn't imagine the hurt if I let you walk away from me. I want to be the one you wake up with, the one who can kiss you at anytime and anyplace, the one who holds your hand as you look into the eyes of our firstborn child."

He released my hand for a few moments to open the box. There nestled in the folds of fabric was the most beautiful two carat radiant cut diamond engagement ring I had ever seen. The tears I cried earlier from sadness were yet again flowing freely – only now from happiness.

He looked deep into my eyes and said with his smile that lit up my world, "Sula Mae, you wanna get hitched next year on October 20th?"

There was a lump in my throat the size of Haley's Comet that prevented me from answering a question I had waited for since I was a little girl reading all of those fairy tales. All I managed to do was nod.

I gathered myself before I spoke through a smile, "I think I'll be free that day."

He slowly placed the ring on my finger, and then just as slowly, slid up my body until he was standing in front of me. He placed his hands on either side of my face and kissed me with a passion that comes only from the soul. It was all so overwhelming that I began to swoon.

He held me up and said, "Oh no my Sula Mae, don't pass out on me. I want us both to remember this moment with perfect clarity for the rest of our lives."

Special Thanks

First and foremost I have to thank God, the creator of everything, for blessing me with a talent and passion to write since age six. Without His grace and mercy, this would not be possible. Thanks to all the authors who are in my personal library, several questions that I had were always answered and served as a template to creating this novel. Thanks to my family and special friends for bearing with me through this process. I missed a lot of social events so I could get this done. Thanks for being understanding and mostly, thanks for remaining a friend during the process. Thanks to my Pentagon family for supporting my first published novel "Sex & Sandwiches". Karen Wray was the first to finish reading it, Michelle Bailey was the first person to purchase anything that I've ever written. Carmen, Karen C. and DJ David J. helped put it on the map in DC and Maryland. I'm grateful to all of the book clubs that have supported my work. I love you all. I first started writing this novel in 2002. This is the first novel that I've ever written. All I ever wrote prior to this were screenplays. This novel sat with a publisher for two years until they decided they did not have the resources to publish it. I got very discouraged and put it down for several years, obviously. As more information became available and as I began to surround myself with positive, like-minded individuals was when I revisited the possibility of publishing. Although I never stopped writing, I just had no idea how to make my dream tangible. Thankfully years later, it has finally arrived. So for those who have it in their spirit to write a novel, please just do it. We all have a story within us. It is a lot of hard work and takes dedication, but it can be done. Don't get discouraged and remain persistent. Bless you all and I hope you enjoyed "Searching for Sula"!

Peace and Prosperity,
Tracey